BEHIND THE WALL

A Novella

JANE HARVEY-BERRICK

HARVEY
BERRICK
PUBLISHING

Behind the Wall: A Novella

Copyright © 2017 Jane Harvey-Berrick

First published in the 2016 anthology *Hot for Teacher: 17 stories filled with lust and love*.

This edition, 2017, updated and extended

Cover design by Sybil Wilson / Pop Kitty Designs

ISBN 978-1-912015-52-8
Harvey Berrick Publishing

CONTENTS

DEDICATION

To the man who has been knocked down, but stands up again. To the woman who has been ignored, but demands to be seen. To the child who has been forgotten, but decides to grow up stronger. And to every person who chooses to be positive, even when life is not always kind.

CHAPTER ONE

GARRETT

"Hey, Garrett. Check out the new teacher, man."

Hudson's voice was quiet, so as to not attract attention.

I'd been in this shitty classroom for thirty seconds and I was already itching to leave. It brought back too many bad memories. But getting educated was a condition of trying to get my parole. I could put up with any amount of crap to say goodbye to this hellhole.

I glanced up, sighing inwardly when I saw that Officer Reynolds was with the teacher. Some of the guards were fair, treating us okay, but some, like the asshole in front of me, got off on making us remember which side of the bars we were on. But I figured I'd been inside for five years—Reynolds was in for life, even if he did get to leave every night. Once I was out of this sewer, that was it, done. I was *never* coming back. Not again.

My gaze drifted to the woman standing next to the Warden's poster boy for prison brutality. She looked nervous, but was trying to hide it by standing straight, keeping her chin up, meeting a man's eyes without prejudice or promise.

I turned away. Sure, it was nice to have a female to look at, but anything longer than a quick glance would have Reynolds burning my ass.

Besides, she wasn't my type. I liked my women to look like women: tall, with tits and ass, big hair, lush lips, and a ballsy attitude.

The new teacher was kind of small, although she had a nice rack. Her hair was a pretty auburn color, but it was short, not even chin length. Nothing for a man to grab onto. And not a scrap of makeup. A man dreamed about scarlet lips in a place like this.

I could see her hands shaking as she stood behind the desk, holding onto her schoolbag like it would save her from drowning.

Not in this classroom, sweetheart.

She wouldn't last. She looked as if a stiff breeze would blow her over.

Reynolds rapped his baton on the desk to get our attention, but the only person who jumped was the new teacher. I was amused to see a warm flush rise up her cheeks. I could tell by the irritated glance she threw Reynolds' way that she was annoyed with him as well as herself.

Reynolds looked as though he was about to start one of his lectures, telling us how we was shit and not worth the money spent on keeping our asses in prison, but the woman stepped from behind the desk and started talking.

"Hello, class," she said, walking to the front as her blush faded. "My name is Miss Newsome..."

My mouth dropped open, and every swivel-eyed pervert in the room was transfixed by our new teacher. She had the smallest waist hovering over the biggest ass I'd ever seen. Hourglasses didn't have anything on her. I scrubbed my hands over my face. One hour of sheer hell coming up.

"I wish I did *knew some* her ass," mumbled Cooper from the back of the room, echoing the thoughts of every man here.

"Who said that?" roared Reynolds, stalking down the gap between the desks that were bolted to the floor. "Cooper, you show some goddamn respect or you'll be spending the next six weeks in solitary!"

Reynolds' face had turned a reddish-purple, and I wondered if we'd be lucky enough to watch him stroke out. Movie night had been cancelled for the last month, so the boredom level was at an all-time high.

But then the teacher cleared her throat, her voice stronger although still high pitched with tension.

"As I was saying, my name is Miss Newsome, and I'll be your teacher for the rest of the semester..."

"We ain't got no semesters here," muttered Chiverson. "Just one-to-three for felony assault."

Reynolds growled out another threat.

Miss Newsome ignored him, approaching the front row, giving those lucky bastards a ring-side view of a knee-length charcoal gray skirt stretched tight over those wide hips, and a plain white shirt that did nothing to hide her fuck-me curves.

She was obviously trying to go for spinster, but she'd lucked out on sexy librarian instead.

I was doomed. I'd never pass my GED with her as my teacher. I raised my eyes to the ceiling, praying to some higher power that I definitely didn't believe in.

It was only when the room went silent, no man even breathing, that I realized she'd stopped by my seat.

"Am I boring you already, Mr. ... Garrett?"

I saw her eyes dip to the number printed across my prison scrubs before checking her clipboard for my name.

I didn't know which surprised me more—hearing her say my name, calling me 'mister', or the sass in her voice as she did it. Girl was tougher than she looked.

Yep, screwed. Royally fucking screwed.

I realized that she was still waiting for an answer.

"No," I said, dropping my eyes to her hips, before squeezing my eyelids shut. "I mean, no, ma'am."

"Good!" she said brightly. "I look forward to your full participation in this class."

"Party— what?" asked Jakowski, sitting at the desk next to me, his voice hopeful.

Her eyes softened a fraction as she turned in his direction, and I couldn't help noticing that they were large and brown, like a puppy or Bambi's mom before she got shot.

Ah, shit.

"Participation," she said calmly. "It means that I want everyone to join in during my classes, not sit there thinking about what you're having for dinner."

A soft rumble of amusement rippled through the room. Reynolds looked furious. But then again, that was pretty much his resting bitch-face.

"I'll do my best to keep the lessons interesting," she went on. "But we have a lot of work to get through. I know you're all up to the challenge because you've been specially selected—you guys are my top class."

I looked up at that. I'd never been top of anything, unless it was a hot woman. I saw a lot of the other guys eyeing her with disbelief and mistrust, too.

"I mean it," she said softly, as we all hung on her every word. "Mr. Michaels, the Warden, is very keen that everyone in this class gets their GED. It's my job to make sure that you do. But I'll need your cooperation to achieve that. I promise that I'll make every effort to help you, but you all need to promise me that you'll try, as well. So, I don't want anyone in this classroom sitting silently because they don't understand. If you have a question, you raise your hand. Please remember that you learn by asking questions. Don't be macho about it—ignorance isn't bliss."

I felt her gaze on me again, but I kept my head down.

"Isn't that right, Mr. Garrett?"

I didn't like her picking on me, and I frowned at my rough hands clasped together on the empty desk.

"Answer her, boy!" snarled Reynolds, rapping his baton next to my fingers, making me snatch them away fast.

"Yes, ma'am," I muttered, keeping my eyes fixed on the buttons of Reynolds' uniform to keep from punching the bastard.

Yep, those eighteen months of mandatory anger management classes had gotten through to me: *think first, punch later when you won't get caught.*

Miss Newsome cleared her throat, bringing attention back to her.

I drew in a breath, and as she drifted past me, the faint scent of summer flowers hung in the air. I didn't think she was wearing perfume, so it must have been her shampoo or soap, but whatever it was, the smell was all woman.

I breathed deeply again, feeling a mixture of anger and dizziness at having something so enticing, near but out of reach.

"Those of you who graduate my class will have the opportunity to move on to college-level courses."

At that point, most of us lost interest. We hadn't succeeded in school and we hadn't succeeded in life. What made this college-educated bitch think she could give us anything we needed?

Sensing she was losing us, she went on brightly, her voice a little more shrill than it had been a minute before.

"And I'll be looking out for a teacher's aide as we go on —so maybe you can impress the heck out of me."

Looking around at the bored, disconnected expressions of the other prisoners, it seemed unlikely.

"Okay, so I thought I'd start off with a poem by Oscar Wilde, 'The Ballad of Reading Gaol'."

Her voice gained strength as she read, but fuck me, what a depressing fucking poem. I listened to the rise and fall of her voice, but I tuned out most of the words.

"*I never saw a man who looked*
With such a wistful eye
Upon that little tent of blue
Which prisoners call the sky."

That penetrated—so many times I'd looked up at the patch of sky above the exercise yard and tried to remember what it felt like to be free. Free to stare up at the sky and not have to watch my back at the same time.

From the corner of my eye, I saw a black guy I didn't know raise his hand, making the teacher stutter and pause.

"Yes, Mr. ... Haslett?"

"Ma'am, we already know all about prison. Rather we'd study somethin' else."

Her mouth popped open and her eyes screwed up. Ah hell! Surely she wasn't going to cry? If she did, she'd never put a foot in this classroom again.

"Oh," she huffed, sounding flustered. "Yes, I see."

I was fascinated by a bead of sweat that escaped her hairline, running down her cheek and disappearing into her prim collar.

I expected her to wipe it away with those long, slim fingers. But she acted like she hadn't noticed, even though the classroom was rank with humidity, sweat and failure.

"I just thought..." she waffled on. "I thought ... no, you're right. Well, we could study a poem about love—about love and hate? Would that be better?"

The black guy twitched a shoulder.

"You're the teacher."

Miss Newsome laughed. It was such a bright sound, easy, such a contrast to the tense, angry or bored voices I heard around me the rest of the day.

Something tightened in my chest.

Six months. Six more months, then maybe I can find myself a woman who laughs so free and easy.

I enjoyed the view of Miss Newsome's ass as she walked back to her desk, the rhythmical sway of those full hips, the way her skirt swung around her knees. Pretty fucking mesmerizing.

She started rummaging through her enormous pile of books. Her lips were moving, and I guessed that she was talking to herself.

Her pile was huge, and she was in danger of tipping over. But the thought of her ending ass up across her desk made my prison uniform uncomfortably tight. And if the expressions of the guys around me were anything to go by, she was having the same effect on them.

Miss Newsome had better watch her cute ass and not get caught in an empty classroom with any of these goons. There's only so much restraint a man has. I frowned at the thought of someone violating teacher-lady. No, that pissed me off.

Goddammit! Now I'd feel obliged to keep an eye on her.

I slumped in my seat, sighing heavily, only noticing the stink-eye she gave me when Hudson elbowed me in the ribs again, grinning broadly.

She snapped open the book she was holding like she was

about to shank me with it, and with a final glare, began to read.

"Some say the world will end in fire,
Some say in ice.
From what I've tasted of desire
I hold with those who favor fire.
But if it had to perish twice,
I think I know enough of hate
To say that for destruction ice
Is also great
And would suffice."

She lowered the book, her face flushed, and when she glared in my direction again, I guessed she must still be mad at me. Great.

"The poet, Robert Frost, was inspired by the fourteenth-century Italian poet Dante and his description of Hell. The worst offenders—traitors—are in a fiery hell while bound in ice. And isn't that contradiction an apt description of love?"

There was a moment of silence before anyone spoke.

"That poem is the shit, ma'am!" said a guy to my right. "Like how a woman gets you all hot and angry, then freezes your ass off 'cause you didn't get her the right kind of candy. And how it gets you fired up that she can be so cold, and all you can think of is warming her up till she burning like a Fourth of July firework."

"Yeah, and then you blow your fucking load and it's a loud bang and all over," laughed another guy.

"Watch your damn mouth, Fisher!" Reynolds yelled. "You will respect your teacher and keep your language clean."

"It's fine, really," Miss Newsome said weakly.

Reynolds turned to her slowly.

"With all due respect, *ma'am*, these animals will take

advantage any chance they get. You've got to let 'em know who's boss."

She flushed with anger and embarrassment, but for the rest of the lesson, she could hardly get a word out of anyone; no one wanted to be on the wrong side of Reynolds. No one wanted to end up in solitary on his watch.

It was the quietest poetry discussion that I'd ever seen. And I couldn't even spell party— partycipation...

As the bell rang for chow time, the little teacher looked almost desperate.

"Thank you all for today," she said, smiling like she'd just chewed on a juicy lemon. "I'm afraid there's homework— but nothing too much for the first time. I'd like you all to write a page on the subject of 'the best day of my life'."

Benson raised his hand.

"Was it when you graduated college, Miss?"

"What? Oh no! I mean what was the best day of *your* life?"

Benson stared at her gravely.

"Well, let me see now; I been incarcerated for nineteen years, and might get paroled next winter. I'll have been in stir more than half my life. Ain't been a whole lot of best days."

She blinked rapidly, then gave him a soft smile.

"Maybe you'd like to *imagine* what your best day would be like?"

He stared back at her, then nodded solemnly.

"I reckon I'd like that just fine."

She smiled with relief.

"Good, good. And the same goes for the rest of you. If you want to imagine your best day instead, that's okay by me."

As we filed out of the room, Reynolds watching our

backs like the answer to the Universe was written on them, the teacher gave us each a lined sheet of paper and a blunt pencil.

"Write small," she teased.

When she handed me my paper, her smile slipped.

And I can't tell you how bad it hurt that she'd smile for every motherfucker in here, but not for me.

CHAPTER TWO

Ella

I filled a large glass with white wine from the fridge, kicked off my shoes, and slumped onto the sofa.

That had to be the longest day of my entire life. It certainly felt like it—I thought it was never going to end. Dear God! What made me think that working in a prison was a good idea?

I blamed my liberal, do-gooder parents, telling me I could go out and change the world, like some modern day Maria Montessori or Dorothea Dix. Although the extra pay and job security of my current employment was nice, too. Working in prisons paid more than working in a regular high school.

But there were downsides. Of course there were.

I was supposed to educate a group of men who leered and ogled each time I bent over, making sexist and inappropriate comments at every opportunity. Not only that, but I'd been given a bodyguard whose idea of warm and cuddly was...

I shook my head. Officer Reynolds didn't have a warm

and cuddly bone in his body. Having him in my classroom had been a disaster. The man was a monster. And I mean that in the truest sense of the word. I could tell by the cold gleam in his eyes that he wanted to use that baton on somebody, instead of just rapping it on the desk every five minutes.

Contrary to what he, and everyone else in the prison seemed to think, I wasn't a shrinking violet. I'd survived six years teaching public school in Baltimore. Definitely not for the faint-hearted.

And I'd started to connect with the men—I know I had. I'd listened to them and they'd listened to me. The Robert Frost poem had got them thinking, got them talking, until that baboon Reynolds effectively shut them down.

I needed to talk to the Warden about having a different officer in my classroom. I knew that I had to have a guard —I wasn't so naïve as to think I didn't need someone at my back—but lessons weren't going to work if the men were too intimidated to speak.

I also had to consider something else: they might need what I could offer, but they didn't want to need me or anyone else, and resentment was already high. They hadn't volunteered for that classroom, they'd been selected, just as I told them. The Warden wanted to improve the prison's dire record on education. But it was more than that: I didn't want to fail these men. Yes, they were criminals, but I was liberal enough to think, *there, but for the grace of God*.

I sighed. Studies had shown that correctional education reduced recidivism by forty-three percent. I could be a part of that.

I was lucky to have been born into a middle class family where tertiary education was the norm, not the exception; where a college fund was started before I was a year old; where there was enough food on the table; and gun ownership was linked to hunting with your buddies on a weekend, not crime.

I'd been fortunate, not desperate.

I shuddered, thinking of the hostility I saw in the men's eyes—some of them, anyway. Especially that man Garrett. God, the way he looked at me! Like I was a fluffy little lamb and he was the big bad wolf, ready to rip me to pieces.

And he was a good-looking asshole, too. I'm sure that on the outside, he'd be one of those men who preyed on women—in the sense that he played with them—a different woman in his bed each night, no doubt. He was too handsome to be anything other than a player.

I wondered what he'd done to get locked up in Nottoway Correctional Center. But Warden Michaels had assured me that it was better not to know what any of them had done. He said only the senior staff had that information, because that way it was easier to give everyone a fair chance, to treat them equally. Knowing what they'd done, what they were capable of doing, it would be impossible to forget.

He was right. And Nottoway was level three security. They weren't the worst criminals, but they weren't tree-huggers either.

On the other hand, if they were nearing parole after a long sentence, like Benson, who knew what serious crimes lurked in their past. Nineteen years he'd been locked up. *Nineteen!* I couldn't imagine it and I didn't want to.

I shivered, remembering Garrett's intense eyes glaring at me. They were so dark, they'd seemed almost black, and a startling contrast to his light, sandy-colored hair.

I took another sip of wine, stretching out my toes and yanking my shirt-tails out of my waistband, unzipping my skirt and pushing it down my legs, then ripping off the constricting pantyhose, and luxuriating in the cool temperature of my air-conditioned apartment.

Nottoway had been incredibly sweaty, and my shirt had been soaked. By the end of the first lesson, the back must have been almost see-through, showing my bra. I'd had to keep my jacket on all afternoon. I was definitely switching to darker colors from now on, even if that seemed kind of depressing.

I'd received strict instructions about what I could and couldn't wear: no makeup, no perfume, no jewelry, no skirts above the knee, no hint of cleavage. I wasn't to give prisoners pens or anything not approved personally by the Warden. Pencils were to be blunt, because a sharpened pencil could be a weapon.

I thought that one was a bit bizarre—any enterprising villain could make a pencil sharp, should he wish to do so. I shuddered at the thought of a needle-pointed pencil aimed at my jugular. But I was abiding by the rules, no matter how odd they seemed.

I wondered what the men were doing now. Having dinner? Free time in front of the TV? Doing chores? I wondered what *he* was doing now.

Of all the imponderables I'd considered before applying to teach a group of adults who happened to be incarcerated —and many disaffected—what I hadn't expected was a man who sauntered from my classroom as if he was going for a beer after work with a friend. He passed my desk without a single glance, and I'd caught the faint aroma of sweat and cigarette smoke.

He was tall with broad shoulders, but even the ugly orange prison-scrubs hadn't been able to hide a runner's whip-hard body. He didn't have the weightlifting bulk that a lot of men turned to in prison; gym time helping to beat the boredom, but also useful for protecting yourself in fights.

But his arms, when he'd crossed them in front of his chest, had been strong, the biceps bulging. Although most of the guys looked fit, even the older ones. I guessed that other than working out, there wasn't a lot to do. And these men didn't strike me as avid readers. Something I'd hoped to change, but now seemed like a vain wish.

I'd caught him watching me once or twice, but always looking away quickly. Which was odd, because being the teacher and commanding attention—or attempting to—it automatically gave the men permission to stare at me. Most of them had taken full advantage of that, but not him. Which was one of the reasons that I'd made a point of checking that he was actually listening to me, and not day dreaming of ... I had no idea what a man like that dreamed about. I probably didn't want to know.

But every now and then, I'd caught a glimpse. His sandy hair was at least three months past needing a haircut, and curled over his collar, dropping across his face, hiding and revealing those dark, dangerous eyes.

I shook my head, as if the action could shake loose the disturbing image. I pushed the thought away. I had a date this evening and I needed to get ready.

I wished I hadn't agreed to meet my best friend Becky for a drink, but at the time she'd suggested it, I thought it would be nice to have something to look forward to after a day spent teaching prisoners. But now all I wanted to do was have a long soak in a hot bath and crawl into bed in my most comfortable and aged pajamas.

Two hours later, I perked up considerably when I saw her sitting at a table in our favorite bar, two Mimosas in front of her.

Her eyes brightened when she saw me, and she leapt up to give me her usual bone-crushing hug.

"Yay! You survived your first day!" she cheered. "I

bought Mimosas to celebrate. So how was it? Are you going back for day two?"

I laughed, the pressure of the day falling away.

"It was ... different. Definitely an experience. And challenging ... very challenging."

"But you're going back?"

"Yes, I can really make a difference teaching these men. If I do my job right, they could actually leave prison with their high school diplomas. It could be the fresh start they need."

She raised one eyebrow.

"You can do that in public school—it doesn't have to be in a prison."

"I know ... it's just ... I feel like the system failed these guys once and ... I don't know..." I sighed. "Bleeding heart liberal—I blame my parents."

Becky gave me a half-smile.

"Just don't have too high expectations. Yes, the system fails some people, but some people choose to fail. You can't save the whole world, Ella."

"I know. I sound incredibly naïve, but that's how I feel about it. Anyway, I'm going to give it a go. If it doesn't work out, I won't be afraid to walk."

Becky looked skeptical.

"El, I've known you ten years—in that time, you've never given up on anything you set your mind to."

I gave a dry laugh.

"There's always a first time."

"Yes, there is. No one is going to say 'I told you so'."

I laughed even louder at that.

"Okay, fine. *Everyone* you know is going to say it." She sighed. "Just be smart about it. Do you have a guard with you? They're protecting you, right?"

I rolled my eyes and let out a groan.

"Ye-es! But the corrections officer they gave me is scarier than most of the inmates. He interrupts my lessons every five minutes by rapping his baton on the desk, and he called them 'animals' in front of them! I can't teach with him around. I'm going to ask for someone else."

Becky looked dismayed.

"He really called them animals?"

"Yes! It was horrible. He said I had to let them know who's boss."

"Well, he's not wrong about that ... are they animals?"

"Becky!"

"I'm just asking!"

"They were mostly pretty well behaved. A bit stare-y, and they were all ogling my boobs or ass."

She smiled and raised an eyebrow.

"Can't blame them for that, honey. They're only human ... human males, that is. Hell, *I* stare at your awesome boobs and bootilicious ass, and I'm straight and female."

I giggled as the Mimosa warmed my stomach.

"I know it's not going to be easy. How can I deliver outstanding lessons when the Warden told me that two of my students have pending court cases and most of the others are nearing parole? They could disappear from class any day." I frowned. "But he also told me that several of them have children, so they want to get their GED to be good role models for once."

Becky nodded. When we'd taught together in public school, we ran a program for parents to improve their literacy skills. That had gotten me interested in teaching adults in the first place.

"There was this one guy though, Garrett," I went on. "He looked dangerous. He kept shooting me these angry looks, like he hated every second of being in my classroom and wanted to be nowhere near me. He was kind of scary. Good-looking asshole, you know?"

"Not really. Good-looking how?"

"All intense dark eyes and messy blond hair. Oh, and a killer body. I don't mean killer, like killer. Although ... maybe. It's possible..."

"Oh my God!"

"No, but seriously," I rambled, "he was built. Really nice arms, and tall, really tall."

Becky gawped.

"Are you seriously telling me that you're crushing on a prisoner?"

"Of course not! The opposite. I'm saying he was scary."

"So the scary prisoner is good-looking and built, and throwing you all these intense, dark stares?"

"When you say it like that ... but, no ... he kind of gives me the creeps."

My brain was buzzing from the alcohol and lack of food. Had Garrett creeped me out? Maybe, a little. But he hadn't said or done anything inappropriate; he hadn't done anything at all. I felt faintly guilty, like I was doing him a disservice by bad-mouthing him to Becky.

But then she ordered another round of Mimosas, and I forgot about Garrett.

For a while.

CHAPTER THREE

GARRETT

I slept like shit. For one thing, Hudson was having nightmares again. He had one most nights, although they'd gotten worse since he'd been told that he'd be up for parole soon.

I asked him about that: he said outside had too much free space. I think he felt safer inside because of all the rules and restrictions. It reminded him of being in the Army, the only time that he'd been happy.

Fuck knows why. I hated being told what to do every hour of every day: when to eat, when to sleep, when to shit. I couldn't wait to get out.

I casually suggested that he see the prison shrink, but he freaked out at that idea, and I had the black eye and bruised ribs to prove it.

But it wasn't just his yelling that kept me awake. I'd been thinking about that sweet and ripe little teacher, and how seeing her in that shitty classroom was like feeling the sun on my face after a long dark winter. But I also knew that she'd taken an instant dislike to me. And for once, I could honestly say that I hadn't done anything. A woman usually waited until *after* I'd slept with her to hate me.

Yeah, I knew it was possible to piss a woman off by just breathing too much air when they was mad at you, but she'd been angrier with me than the guys who mouthed off and disrespected her. I didn't get it. And I hated feeling dumb.

I thought again about her stupid, lame-ass assignment. I had two choices: write it, like she wanted—make up some bullshit about rainbows and unicorns—or I didn't. But if I didn't get a passing grade in her class, I'd be sent to work in the prison's kitchens again dumping slop cans, or end up being dorm janitor for 40¢ an hour, which meant cleaning up the disgusting showers and the shitters after thirty guys had used them, sweeping up the cigarette butts and tobacco spit in the day room, and a hundred other crappy, stomach-churning chores for less money than just about any other job in prison.

The Warden had made it clear to each of us on the GED program that a failing grade would mean being given the shittiest jobs and loss of privileges, like TV and showers. And we weren't supposed to let the teacher know that either. So I guess she'd be allowed to think like she was all shiny and new with us, motivating our sorry asses, when the truth was something else. A big fat shitty something else.

Right now I had to work thirty hours a week on the prison farm. It was okay. I got to be outside a lot, even though I froze my butt off in winter and cooked my ass in summer. And it was one of the most popular jobs because you could get extra food sometimes. I heard one of the guards say that the hard work was supposed to make us less aggressive. I wanted to tell him that letting us out of prison would make us less aggressive, but I kept my mouth shut.

We grew fruit and vegetables that went to the prison

kitchen, and had a large barn for chickens. I didn't like cleaning out them chickens—the smell of ammonia made my eyes water and breath hack up in my chest.

I'd rather have worked in the auto shop like I did in my last prison, but Nottoway didn't have much of an auto program, so I probably wasn't missing out.

The Warden said he'd reduce my hours on the farm to twenty so I had time for school and homework, but it hadn't happened yet. I didn't mind, because fighting boredom was always one of the toughest things about life inside. That, and not letting yourself get too crazy.

I was feeling kind of tired, and the thought of falling into my bunk and catching some ZZZs while Hudson was in the day room was tempting, but when I did close my eyes, I saw the teacher's angry glare aimed at me. And even more frequently, I saw her soft, all-woman curves, and that had me hardening uncomfortably.

All guys jerk off in prison. You have to. It releases some of the tension. Most of us do it at night with the relative privacy of darkness, even though you know there are thirty guys doing the same thing within a few yards of you, or if you have a cellmate, within a few feet.

You do it quick and you do it quiet, but you can still hear other men slapping their skin. It freaked me out when I went inside the first time in juvie, but it's one of those sick, twisted things that you get used to in prison. Like turning a blind eye if someone else is getting beat up, because you're just glad it's not you.

Some guys did it out in the open if there weren't any guards around. Mostly they were homos, but not all. Some got off on being seen. Everything is a public performance in a prison. There are no doors in the bathrooms, so if you're on the john, everyone knows your shit stinks, same as theirs.

It's not like any prison movie you see in here—no one has your back unless you join a gang. And that has its own price. I always hung on my own. Most people will respect that after you show you're not gonna take their shit—maybe take a beat down instead, if you have to. I hung with Hudson a little, him being my cellmate and all, but he was a crazy motherfucker and I didn't want to get pulled into his brand of nuts.

I unfolded the sheet of paper that I'd been given, smoothing it out so it stayed flat for me to write on. I'd already sharpened my pencil against the edge of my metal bunkbed so at least I could write with it now. But words wouldn't come.

What could I say to a nice, clean woman like her? The best day of my life? I hoped that I hadn't had it yet, because otherwise that would mean I had a helluva lot of shit still to come.

Yeah, I'd had some good times, like when the Miro sisters had gotten some quality coke and we'd all gotten high and fucked our brains out. Definitely wasn't going to be sharing *that* memory. Plus, I'd ended up with a killer nosebleed from snorting too much of that shit.

And I couldn't tell her about the time I managed to hotwire a 1991 Ferrari Testarossa and took her up to 145 mph before the cops caught me. One of a series of car-related stunts that got me landed in here.

So if I couldn't tell her about my life, what could I tell her? It would have to be some made-up shit.

I thought about that for a while. Yeah, I could dream, same as any man in stir. We all dreamed about the day we'd be released. Well, maybe not Hudson—it gave him nightmares. But like I said, he was crazy.

And I'd been thinking about getting out a lot lately, now that I could be paroled as soon as six or seven months.

What was I going to do with my sorry-ass life? I knew that if I went home to the old neighborhood I'd be back in prison within a year; two if I was lucky.

Breaking the rules in school had turned to breaking the laws when I got older, and sooner or later that shit catches up with you. What seems real funny when you're twelve is a lot less funny when you're standing before a judge who wants to send you to juvie for eight months. So you act like the big man and take your licks, but inside you're dying just a little bit more.

I was getting old. I'd just spent another birthday in prison—my thirtieth. I didn't want this to be my life. My dreams had gotten smaller as I'd grown older. Now, I just wanted a nice place to live, nothing fancy, but clean and all mine, with a door I could lock myself and the keys stashed in my pocket; a steady job in an auto shop, maybe buy myself a banged up Shelby and fix it up for a hobby; have a regular woman, someone who wore her skirts a decent length and kept her pussy just for me. You know, small stuff, small dreams.

But even those seemed impossible with my record. I'd be leaving prison with no home, no job, no woman, and no future. Guys like me don't get happily ever after. If we're lucky—which we're usually not—we get a job that pays minimum wage or by the hour, and drink ourselves to death worrying about paying the rent on a shitty apartment or a shittier trailer. Like my old man.

But I had to try. I had to, or staring at cell walls would be the next fifty years of my life. And who the fuck wants to live like that?

So I scooted back on my lumpy mattress, leaning against the bare wall, the concrete feeling cool against my sweaty back, and I picked up my pencil, thinking hard, thinking about what life could be like if I dared to dream.

. . .

Ella

It was my third day at Nottoway, and my second session with the GED class.

Day two had been teaching basic literacy skills to a different group of prisoners, and that had its own challenges. For one thing, adults don't like admitting they don't know their alphabet, and recent experience had taught me that showing any sort of weakness in prison, made you a target. So I had to handle the group carefully.

I'd ended up devising a lot of my own resources, because I couldn't use materials made for kindergarteners. 'A' was not for Apple, but the Ace of Spades. 'B' was not for Baby, but Baseball. And so on.

There was a lot of aggression in that group, but luckily I'd been assigned a different corrections officer, a man named Martinez, and he'd had a calming effect on the prisoners. It really, really helped.

I'd also had a quiet word with the Warden to see if I could get rid of Reynolds from the other group. He hadn't been happy about it, but I pointed out that if he wanted his GED group to make the grade, I needed to be helped, not hindered. After that veiled threat, he'd promised to switch the officers around.

Today, I was going to continue the discussion of *Fire and Ice*, but maybe try to steer it away from the sexual connotations I'd inadvertently initiated, and get them talking more about love and hate in general terms, as well as the structure and economy of the poem's words.

Although in all honesty, the most useful part for them would be when I got to the section of the curriculum where I taught them life skills. After all, what interest would a forty year old man have in interpreting a poem by Robert

Frost when he was serving out the last two years of a dozen he'd gotten for armed robbery? Okay, I didn't know what the men were in for, but the core of my point was valid. This was part of the GED, but so was teaching them how to balance a check book, pay taxes, or talk them through obtaining a business license so they could actually set up their lawn-cutting service or handyman business, and make a success of their lives when they left.

I was relieved when I was escorted to my classroom by a taciturn corrections officer named Wilson. He wasn't interested in talking to me, but he didn't seem like the bullying type either. I hoped.

I stood by the classroom door, welcoming every student, using names where I could remember them. But when Garrett sauntered in without looking at me, I felt my skin prickle and overheat.

Damn the man! He hadn't even looked at me—and I was trying to set a pleasant tone for the lesson. I wasn't going to let him undermine me.

"Welcome, everyone! Thank you for coming back."

I grinned at them, letting them know that I was in on the joke. There were a few limp smiles, but it was a start.

"First, I'll ask Mr. Benson to collect your essays from Monday. Please make sure that you've written your name at the top. I hope you all had a chance to write something, even if it was just a few lines..."

"Now you tell us!" groaned the man sitting next to Garrett. "If I'd known you only wanted a few lines, I wouldn't have busted my ass, pardon my French."

I laughed lightly.

"The more you wrote, the better grip I'll get on where you're at academically, Mr. ... Hudson."

I ignored the loud whisper from the back with someone saying they wouldn't mind me getting a grip on them.

Officer Wilson cleared his throat, but he didn't pull out his baton or otherwise interrupt the lesson.

But I felt a little jumpy when I saw Garrett's eyes narrowed in my direction.

The essays were placed on my desk and the man named Hudson winked at me as he walked past. But as he went to sit down, Garrett yanked out the chair so Hudson fell to the floor.

"What the fuck, man?" snarled Hudson, leaping to his feet and clenching his fists.

Garrett stared at him coolly, not even moving an inch.

"Settle down, Hudson," said my bodyguard calmly. "Garrett, anymore of that shit and you and me will be having words."

Garrett leaned back in his chair, a smirk on his handsome face.

I was seething at his behavior, but carried on regardless, refusing to look in his direction for the rest of the lesson. I'd never let a student get to me like this before. The asshole had one more chance, and then I was kicking him out of my class. And I suspected that his last chance would be the essay ... if he'd even attempted it.

I sailed through the rest of the lesson on a cloud of self-justification, but managed to engage a good number of my students, as well. I wondered if it was too early to get them writing their own poetry. Probably. I'd assess what their literacy skills were before I decided about that.

I needed to pick a classic piece of literature to study with them first; I'd hedge my bets by choosing something that had been turned into a movie, as well.

The classroom was far too hot again, and the students' responses were muted by the heavy humidity, rank with body odor that permeated the air. I watched Garrett out of the corner of my eye as he pushed his shaggy hair out of his face, sweat beading on his forehead.

At least this time I'd dressed more appropriately to hide my own sweaty state. I was wearing a navy blue golf t-shirt and pale gray wide-legged pants.

I usually wore medium heels when I was teaching, to give me a bit of height, but I couldn't do that in a prison: too feminine, and a spike heel could be used as a weapon.

It was a learning curve for me as well as my students.

At the end of the lesson, I was pleased and relieved when a few of the men mumbled their thanks, and Mr. Benson even stopped to ask me a question.

"Miss, this Robert Frost dude—he a dead white man, yeah?"

"Well, yes. He died in 1963."

"Figures."

"Ah, which part?" I asked, puzzled.

"Waal, in school the poets they taught were always both of them things."

"Actually, I think you'll find that's not quite right on several levels."

"How you figure, Miss?"

"First, Robert Frost had a pretty tough life. His father died when he was eleven, leaving the whole family in poverty. Then his mother died of cancer; his younger sister died in a mental hospital, and both his wife and daughter also suffered from mental illness. And second, there have been many well-known Black poets. Off the top of my head, Maya Angelou, Phyllis Wheatley, Frank Marshal Davis, but one of my favorite poets is Black, living, and British: Benjamin Zephaniah."

"That so?"

"Yes," I said, pleased so many names had come to mind.

"Then how come we never studied them in school?"

My smile fell.

"I really don't know, Mr. Benson. There are a lot of things that I wish were studied in school."

He nodded slowly, then turned to leave.

"Appreciate that, Miss."

The door closed and I was left in silence. I glanced up at Officer Wilson, and saw the tiniest smile on his face.

"Think I learned something, too," he said, as he escorted me from the room.

I felt like I'd run a marathon and won a boxing match. I was exhausted but happy.

I can do this!

But when I got home, my happy, positive vibe vanished like morning mist as I read through the men's essays.

The level of literacy was lower than I'd been led to believe, but worse than that, half of the essays were pornographic, and it felt as if they'd been written to put me in my place. Some were so unpleasant, I couldn't bring myself to finish reading them.

I sighed, and tossed aside another so-called essay. It had been my own fault for giving them such vague guidelines. I should have known better—and I would for the future.

I cringed when I picked up Garrett's essay, or 'Prisoner 97813' as he'd written at the top of the sheet in large, ungainly block letters.

But as I read, my eyes opened wide.

> *I don't know what a best day is. Maybe its an ordinary day where at the end of it you fall asleep with a clear conshunse. Maybe I've had my best day but I hope not becuz that would be a crying shame. So Im going to imajin my best day like you said.*
>
> *Today is the best day of my life becuz its the day I walk out these prison doors and never look back. I*

dont look back at the high fences or the thick concreet walls. I dont look back at the guards or the other prisoners. I walk out a free man.

The sun is shining but theres a breeze. Not to hot. Not to cold. The air smells real good. Fresh and clean. I never smelled such good clean air. I close my eyes and I can feel the sun on my face like its washing away all the dirt and bad stuff I seen.

But best of all is the silence. Its so quite out here. So still. If I lissen real hard I think Ill here birds singing like I never hered them befor.

I think of all the things Im going to do now Im a freeman. Ill have money in my pocket becuz this is my dream. Enough to buy a beer or three. Not to get blasted just to get a nice buz. And Ill have a nice place to go home to. Ive got a car but Im going to walk just becuz I can. Ill walk like Im free. Strolling, not looking over my shoulder. Not rushing or nothing. Just easy.

And maybe when I look up she will be waiting for me. Shell smile at me. A big smile just for me. And I no shes a good woman and so dam butiful. And my heart beats faster becuz its been so long. So long since I held a woman in my arms. And not just any woman but this woman. And im going to take her home and love her the way she deserves but right now all I want to do is hold her and feel her softness against my hardness. Feel her curves against me and look down into her soft brown eyes and say your my woman.

That would be the best day of my life. But I no it wont be like that becuz dreams arent real but I think it would be nice if they were.

I laid down the piece of paper, shocked to my core. It

was not at all what I'd expected. His writing moved me in ways I couldn't explain. There was hope and hopelessness, desire and despair. So much raw emotion.

But I knew one thing: I'd completely misunderstood Prisoner 97813. I'd treated him like the stereotype that I was supposed to abhor. I'd assumed he wasn't interested in bettering himself, that he wasn't listening to my lessons. But I'd been so very wrong. His air of indifference wasn't the real man. It was a mask he used to hide behind.

The man who wrote those words felt everything deeply, thought about things deeply. This was a man I wanted to know more. I was surprised by the tiniest prick of jealousy toward the unnamed woman. I wondered who she was, hoping that she'd be someone who could bring out the best in him. And from an academic level, I should be jumping for joy—I could teach a man like this. I could really help him.

I read through the page of writing again, moved by the simple joy of the things he wanted to experience—things most of us were too busy to notice: the sun on our skin, the breeze in our hair, friendship, companionship. Love. All his longings expressed in simple but moving language.

But also his sense of loss and defeat that none of this would be in his future. My heart broke a little for Prisoner 97813.

He *had* been listening.

CHAPTER FOUR

GARRETT

Hudson grabbed the front of my prison uniform and slammed me up against the cell wall, hard.

I let my hands hang limply by my side because he had a right to be pissed at me.

"What the fuck was that about, shithead? Why the fuck you send my ass to the floor?"

"Seemed like the thing to do at the time," I grinned at him.

My answer wound him up even more and I felt his hands tightening on my shirt.

"The fuck you mean?"

"If you're gonna hit me, get to it. But if you're just gonna mess with my clothes, ask me on a date first."

He jumped back like he'd been stung, swearing as I laughed my ass off. He collapsed on my bunk, half-annoyed, half-amused.

"What's with you, man? You're acting psycho, and I'm supposed to be the crazy one in this cell."

He sat up suddenly, awareness on his face.

"In fact I'm thinking you've been acting weird since we started lessons with little Miss Awesome-ass." His smile grew as he stared at me. "That's it! I'm right, aren't I? You've got a boner for teacher!"

"It's not like that," I grumbled, annoyed that I was busted.

"That's why you dumped my ass on the floor, 'cause she was smiling at me and not you. Maybe she thinks I'm prettier than you," and he let out a loud laugh.

The guy had a face that looked like it had been kicked by a mule.

"Yeah, yeah, whatever," I said, sounding like a whiny little bitch.

He fixed me with a stare, still smiling.

"Bro's before ho's, man! Guys like us learn that in grade school."

"She's different."

"Ah, right. You think she's gonna educate your ass in private lessons, that it?"

"No! It's just ... you ever meet a woman like her before? Decent?"

He shrugged.

"Sure. Pussy is pussy, however you dress it up."

A rush of anger jetted through me. I should have known better than to try and talk about this shit with Hudson. Guy was whacked.

But then his tone eased half a degree.

"I'm just yanking your tail. I get it, I do. She makes you want more than this," and he waved his arms toward the barred window. "I feel you, man."

And that was the trouble. She made me want more than I could ever realistically have. Ever.

And that was depressing as fuck.

. . .

Ella

Day five at Nottoway Correctional Center. Day three with my GED class. And Garrett.

I felt like I owed him an apology, but I didn't want to show weakness either.

In the end, I decided to play it straight and treat him like everyone else—neither friendlier nor less.

But when he walked into my classroom, I had to admit that my heart beat just a little faster, even though he didn't look at me once. But I understood now, so I didn't let it bother me either.

"Good morning, everyone," I began, once they'd all shuffled to their seats and Officer Wilson had closed the door. "This is our third class together, so it's time to get serious. All but one of you turned in a paper. That person has been spoken to and will not miss assigned homework again without a doctor's note—or you'll be out of this class. You know who you are," and I stared around, meeting as many eyes as would look at me.

"Only half of you finished the assigned homework to an acceptable standard," I continued. "I'm sure the ones who didn't can guess why. This is a classroom, not a pornographic film studio. Anymore of that behavior, you'll be asked to leave this class and I'll turn your essays over to Warden Michaels. So, to those people I'll say you've used up your one chance with me. To the half of you who received a passing grade—which is C or above—well done. And to the man who achieved B+, excellent work and I look forward to your continued achievement and future progress."

They all stared at me like I'd just grown a second head, and then from the back of the room I heard,

"That was freakin' hot!"

I ignored it and carried on.

"Mr. Garrett, would you hand back the papers, please?"

His head jerked up, his dark eyes locking with mine. Reluctance oozed from his body as he slid from his chair and sauntered toward me, aversion in every step.

I gave him a small smile and handed over the papers with his on top, the B+ circled in red.

I didn't want to point him out in front of the others, but I did want him to know how much I liked what he wrote and that I appreciated his efforts.

For a moment, his attitude of disinterest slipped, and I saw his eyes widen at the grade I'd given him. For the briefest second, a small, pleased smile curled the edges of his lips, and then it was gone.

But I'd seen it ... and I'd seen *him*.

The rest of the lesson went well, and I pushed them hard, going over some of the basic rules of grammar, as well as how to structure future essays.

Then I introduced them to my chosen text.

"We're going to be studying *Hunger* by the Norwegian writer Knut Hamsun."

"Oh, man, I seen that movie!" said Fisher. "It's got lesbo vampires in it and shit."

I settled them down quickly.

"No, that's *The Hunger*—something completely different. The book I'm talking about tells the story of a young man who is a writer, but unable to make a living through his writing, and is slowly starving on the streets of Oslo, that's Norway's capital city. He's not a sympathetic character, but impulsive and chaotic. It was written over a hundred years ago, but feels very modern with its stream-of-consciousness style. Who can tell me what that means?"

There was some discussion about that, then Benson answered, "Yeah, that's writing down whatever shit comes out of yo' mouth."

"Pretty much, yes. But it's an artificial construct because in reality that would be a very boring read. But we'll get to that and yes, before you ask, there is a movie version."

I didn't tell them that it was made in the sixties, black-and-white, and that they'd have to read the subtitles. I wasn't that brave.

Baby steps.

Garrett

I only heard about half of what she said. I'd turned my paper face down so Hudson couldn't see my grade, but it was there, burning a hole in my desk. She'd given *me* the top grade in the whole damn class.

I'd never gotten anything like that in my life. Not ever. I had to fight back the smile that kept threatening to turn me into a grinning idiot. The warmth of pride flowed through my body, making me feel calm and energized all at the same time.

It was a dangerous feeling, because it made dreams seem possible.

I glanced up at her, watching her face full of animation and passion. She gave that to a bunch of prisoners, guys from the streets. I admired her, and I was jealous as fuck of every asshole that she smiled at or spoke to. I wanted it all for myself.

I wanted *her*.

Ella

At the end of the lesson, the men filed out, talking about the work, talking about what we'd studied today. It was a great feeling, knowing that they felt inspired by something beyond these prison walls.

"Mr. Garrett," I said quietly as he stood to leave, "if I could have a moment, please."

He looked surprised and not entirely happy about it, but sank down into his seat again without argument.

I waited until everyone had left the room, except my bodyguard who was lounging patiently at a short distance.

Before I could second-guess myself, I sat down next to Garrett, noting with amusement that his whole body stiffened and he moved away from me fractionally. His essay was tightly rolled and held in his fist.

"You did really well on your assignment," I began. "I was impressed."

I waited for him to comment, but his eyes were fixed on the empty desk.

"So, I was wondering," I continued. "You know that I mentioned I'd be looking for a teacher's aide in this class ... well, I thought you might like the job. What do you think?"

His head jerked up, and those dark, hungry eyes met mine.

"Why me?" he asked, his voice low and rough.

I kept my tone as even as possible, trying to ignore the fact that our thighs were just inches apart. Not wanting to admit that this man affected me.

"You scored the highest mark on the assignment and..." I cleared my throat nervously as he continued to stare. "I liked what you wrote—I like the way your mind works."

His eyes widened with surprise, then narrowed again with suspicion.

"You like my ... mind?"

"It's up to you," I said briskly, starting to stand. "Because it will take extra time to help me with lessons, the Warden is prepared to reduce your duties elsewhere. And I believe there are extra privileges that he'll discuss with you."

I turned to walk away, but Garrett laid his hand on my arm, stopping me in my tracks. His fingers rested there for a second, burning a brand into my skin, and then he dropped his hand.

"Thank you," he murmured.

"You'll take the job?"

He nodded once and looked away.

"Good."

As I watched him leave the classroom, his mask firmly in place, I felt nervous about my decision.

Officer Wilson watched him leave, then turned his assessing eyes to me.

"A reluctant student."

I gave him a wry smile. "And by 'reluctant' you mean...?"

"Ah, well ... he didn't exactly get along with the teacher in his previous prison."

"Oh! What happened?"

"He threw a chair at the wall. It bounced off and hit another student, started a fight, damn near a riot. But he wasn't trying to hurt the teacher."

"Oh."

My heart thundered as I thought about all the times I'd be one-to-one with Garrett now I'd made him my aide.

"We'll look after you, Miss, don't worry," said Wilson. "Gotta keep that pretty face of yours safe."

"Anything else I should know?"

"He transferred out of a level four facility a few months ago—and he'd twenty-four months of good behavior prior to his transfer, although he wasn't allowed back in a classroom. He's got a temper on him, but he's not dangerous: pissed at the world and with a bad attitude. The usual. If anyone can reach him, you can."

As a teacher in Baltimore public school, I was proud of my reputation with the hard-to-teach pupils. Every day was a new challenge, but one that I gladly accepted. Most days, anyway.

When Garrett walked into my class, I hadn't been expecting anything other than the macho posturing that high school juniors and seniors always seemed to wear. It hadn't intimidated me then and I wasn't about to let it start now.

But as I drove home that afternoon, an internal war waged bitterly, and I second-guessed my decision the whole way.

He's violent.

I wondered again what he'd done to earn his incarceration, and whether or not I should find out.

But there was more to it than that. A lot more.

Garrett *had* done the best work, but I knew nothing about him, except for those few honest words on a sheet of paper. And yet somehow, I'd come to care for him. His hopeless, hope-filled words had touched something inside me.

And for that reason alone, I should stay as far away from him as possible.

But I was a teacher and a professional. I should be fair and objective.

On the other hand, I didn't know any other teachers who went to college planning to end up in jail.

CHAPTER FIVE

GARRETT

"So, you're going to be teacher's pet now?"

Hudson jeered when I sat down on my bunk.

"Fuck off," I replied, without much heat.

I stretched out on the hard mattress and rested my hands behind my head, staring up at Hudson's sagging mattress but seeing nothing. I wished I could be alone with my thoughts, but there's no privacy in prison—not even in your head.

Hudson jumped down and shoved my feet out of the way so he could sit next to me.

"You're gonna get your ass in trouble if you mess with her—you'll fuck up your parole."

"I'm not going to mess with her," I said testily.

He didn't reply, but when I opened my eyes, his expression was worried.

"What the fuck do you care?" I asked roughly.

"Man, the world is an ugly motherfucking place," he said, frowning. "But suddenly you're seeing sunshine and rainbows. Fuck's sake, you'll be singing show tunes next. You gotta see this for what it is."

"And that is?"

"Passing the GED is your ticket outta here!" he half-yelled. "You keep on with all those long, meaningful glances at Miss Awesome-ass, and Wilson might wake the fuck up and report you. I'm telling you, brother, keep your cock in your pocket and don't fuck up."

I groaned. It really didn't help by talking about Miss Newsome and my dick in the same sentence.

"Come on, you sad fucker," he laughed. "Let's do some reps."

He dragged me off the bunk by my ankles and let my ass hit the floor. Definitely payback.

Then we spent the next hour doing pull-ups using the bunkbed frame, pushups and crunches.

It was one way to pass the evening.

But it didn't erase the memory of her sitting so close to me, the scent of flowers filling the air around us, the heat of her body, the feel of her soft skin under my rough, callused hand.

My dick hardened uncomfortably, and I knew I'd have another sleepless night where even jerking off wouldn't help. Much.

Ella

When I walked into the classroom escorted by Officer Wilson, Garrett was waiting for me.

This time, he acknowledged me as I entered, standing up quickly, his dark eyes darting to Wilson and back to me.

"Good morning, Garrett," I said pleasantly, as my pulse began to race.

Act normal, my brain screamed at my treacherous body.

"Ma'am," he said quietly.

I waited for him to sit down again, then sat next to him, ignoring his slight movement away from me.

"The focus of today's lesson will be *Hunger* and the character's fall from grace. I think the students will recognize some aspects," I said wryly.

Garrett cracked the faintest smile and shifted in his seat again.

I caught the now familiar scent of cigarette smoke and sweat.

"Do you smoke?" I asked randomly.

He blinked, looking surprised by my unplanned question.

"No."

I waited, but he didn't say anything else. I was disappointed—I'd hoped to build a rapport with him, but that wouldn't be easy if he was monosyllabic.

I sighed and picked up the text book.

"I used to," he said quietly, not looking at me. "Outside. But I can't afford it in here. Smokes cost too much and I don't have the money."

"Oh," I said stupidly. "I'm glad. Smoking is bad for you."

He gave a soft, quiet laugh, his whole face lighting up. He was transformed, seeming younger and gentler. And so beautiful. So very beautiful.

My breath caught in my throat, and I had to look away.

"You ... you smell smoky."

And yes, my IQ seemed to keep dropping.

His skin flushed and he looked down, his smile vanishing.

"I don't mean that you smell bad," I said lamely. "Just ... just smoky."

"I was in the day room at lunchtime," he said softly. "You can smoke in there."

"Oh. Right."

I cleared my throat and opened the textbook.

"We'll be reading the first chapter today, then summarizing it. Everyone will be working in pairs, and I want you to work with Huxley. He has good comprehension skills, but is less able with literacy."

Garrett shifted uneasily.

"I don't spell so good."

"You're not bad, but it's something we can work on. And you can definitely help Huxley while I move around working with other students."

He seemed pensive, but whatever he was going to say was interrupted by Officer Wilson.

"Miss Newsome, I wouldn't recommend you roaming around the classroom—better if you stick to teaching from the front."

I looked up, completely taken aback. Wilson was one of the more progressive guards; I hadn't expected such negativity.

But then Garrett backed him up.

"He's right, ma'am."

He stopped speaking, his mouth tightening.

"What?" I snapped, irritated that these men were trying to tell me how to teach.

I was hardly a newbie.

Garrett grimaced.

"Someone coming up behind you is bad news in prison. Men react. And when you get too close … it's hard to concentrate."

I stared at him in shock, watching his eyes flick across my body rapidly. But not so fast that I didn't see it.

I felt a blush redden my cheeks.

"I see," I said quickly.

I swallowed several times, my throat unaccountably dry, and tried to carry on, my focus shot.

Then someone came to the door to talk to Wilson, and Garrett took the opportunity to lean toward me.

"I'm sorry," he whispered.

I felt the warmth of his breath across my cheek, and for a split second his knee pressed against mine.

He'd spoken just two words, three little syllables, but I felt as if it was so much more. He'd let the mask slip and shown me his real self.

Or maybe I was being naïve. Maybe I just wanted to believe in him, but really I was being played by the ultimate conman. But maybe not.

"Ella. My name is Ella."

His full lips parted, forming a surprised 'O', then he straightened up and moved away from me before Wilson saw him.

As the other prisoners started to enter the room, their curious gazes on me and Garrett sitting so closely together, I stood quickly and resumed my place behind the teacher's desk.

I began the lesson, calmly explaining what we'd be doing today and what I hoped the men would achieve. It was hard teaching from the front when I was used to moving among my students, but I'd been advised by two men who knew what they were talking about, so I paid attention. Instead, I let the men come to me, singly or in pairs, when they wanted to ask a question.

Garrett was good with Huxley, patient and methodical as I watched and listened from a distance, and I knew I'd made the right decision to choose him for my aide. Personal feelings aside.

The lesson was over too quickly and the men filed out. Garrett's eyes met mine as he left, but he didn't smile. If I hadn't seen it for myself an hour ago, I would have believed that he'd never smiled in his whole life.

Garrett

Ella. Ella Newsome.

It fit her—pure, gentle, innocent.

Knowing her name was a new kind of torture. I imagined whispering her name in the dark as I made her fall apart under me.

Ella. *My Ella*.

She wasn't mine by any stretch of the imagination and never would be, but the words were too sweet to ignore, and they echoed in my brain like the crackling heat of midsummer.

I wanted her. I wanted to feel her soft skin under my hands, her silky hair wrapped around my fists, and my dick balls deep inside her slick little pussy.

I groaned as vivid images ran like a porn movie inside my head.

But she was so much more than just a warm, tight body. She cared about teaching us. And no one had ever cared before.

So for her, I'd take my job as teacher's aide seriously. Besides, I'd get some new privileges including an extra shower mid-week and more time in the prison's gym.

And if Ella thought I could help other people, then maybe I wasn't as worthless as I'd always been told.

At first, it was kind of a joke to the other men, and I certainly got my share of ribbing for it during the next few weeks. But then some of the guys from the GED class started coming to me in the day room and asking a question or wanting me to check their work.

It became a regular sight, me sitting with another

prisoner, acting like I was a damn teacher, as we worked through a problem together. And my own reading and writing was improving—just doing it every day helped. Who knew that studying worked?

It was strange, but it felt good, and it soon became the norm and no one bothered us anymore. Well, a few assholes, but once they'd had a taste of my fists, they stuck to name-calling, which was a pussy way of behaving and easy to ignore.

Wilson wasn't my biggest fan, and since Hudson's warning, I'd seen the way he watched me when Ella sat by my side before the start of every lesson.

It was all but impossible not to touch her, but there was nothing I could do about it when she touched me. A brush of her hands, the press of her knee, the tap of her nails on my arm as she emphasized a point.

Every one of those brief, near-innocent touches, was burned in my memory.

And while Wilson watched me, I watched her. She didn't touch the other guys the way she touched me, and that made my heart soar. I honestly thought that my emotions had shriveled up years ago, leaving an angry, bitter man behind. But with her, I was relearning how to feel— some long repressed part of me had stirred. I tried to be as cool as I could with her, but I was falling, caught by wide brown eyes and a passionate heart.

Wilson knew what she did to me, he could see it in my eyes, and he didn't like it. So he watched.

But when he saw me tutoring the other prisoners, he eased up some on the hard expression and warning stares.

And each night I fell asleep dreaming of Ella.

Sweet Ella.

My Ella.

.   .   .

Ella

In the weeks that followed, the highlight of my days were those brief, snatched moments with Garrett.

And, finally, as the weather grew colder and I added cardigans to my dreary prison uniform of slacks and shirts, I dredged up the courage to ask him about his crime.

His lazy gaze slid to me as I held my breath, his expression a mixture of surprised and wary.

Please let it not be anything that changes what I think of him. But the boundaries were blurring, and something that would have been a large *STOP* sign two months ago, was now *proceed with caution*. What was I okay with? What could I tolerate? Was robbery excusable? What about drug offenses? What if it was rape? What if his story was filled with rage and violence?

I shouldn't be asking him...

He turned his eyes to the book on the desk in front of him, mumbling, aware of Officer Wilson watching us closely.

"Cars. I have a ... weakness for nice cars."

"As in stealing them?"

He was a thief.

I didn't know whether to be disappointed or relieved that it wasn't something worse. My moral ground trembled under my feet.

He shrugged.

"I just like driving nice cars. I didn't crash them or anything."

I turned to stare at him in outraged disbelief. But then I saw a smile twitching at the corner of his mouth.

"Oh, you!"

He grinned, looking younger and boyish again.

"I thought stealing from rich folks would pay better— turns out they have nicer cars *and* better security."

I returned his smile and raised an eyebrow.

"Lesson learned?"

"Yes, ma'am," he grinned. Then his expression became serious. "I was young and poor and stupid. I'd already been in juvie for fighting, and I was angry all of the time. I'd been smoking weed..." he shot me a quick look to measure my level of shock, but I just cocked my head to one side, listening. "I'd gotten it into my head to drive to the ocean. I'd never seen it, and I wanted to. So, I thought I'd take this guy's car and drive there. Try to sell it later, I guess." He shrugged. "I got caught before I'd driven a mile, and I punched one of the police officers who arrested me. I don't remember too much about that. I've paid for it. Fuck, I've paid for it. But I'm not that kid anymore either," he said, his voice low and urgent, begging me to believe him. "And I'm not coming back here. Not ever."

"I'm glad to hear it," I said quietly, resting my hand briefly on his arm. "Very glad."

"Are you?"

He gave me an intense look, so many questions in his dark eyes. I wanted to tell him it was going to be okay, but the lie burned on my tongue. I wanted to give him some sort of reassurance, but confusion and cowardice kept me silent.

Then before he could say anything more or I could answer, the other prisoners arrived and it was time to start the lesson.

His frustrated expression matched my own. We never had any time, we never had any privacy. I wanted both—a thought that scared me half to death.

At the end of a long, exasperating day where nothing seemed to go as I wanted, I was happy to shake Nottoway dust from my shoes and head out for a drink with Becky.

"How's it going in stir, sista?" she asked in her best *Orange is the New Black* impression.

"Fine," I mumbled.

"Fine as in I-broke-both-my-legs-but-don't-worry-about-me fine, or fine as in today-sucked-ass-and-I'm-feeling-sorry-for-myself?"

"Probably the latter," I said, unable to stop a tired smile appearing on my face.

"Come tell Aunty Becky all about it, but not before you've had at least one Mimosa."

"Honestly, I don't really feel like drinking. I'll just get all weepy and mopey."

She shook her head and pushed a glass toward me.

"So get weepy and mopey. How's it going with Mr. Hottie-con?"

"He's ... doing well. He makes a great teacher's aide—better than I could have hoped. The other prisoners go to him in between classes. They're all making so much progress."

"That's good then."

"Yes."

"And?"

"And nothing."

"So, you're not fantasizing about the length of his ... parole?"

"Becky!"

"I'm right, aren't I? You're totally crushing on your jailbird boy toy."

"He's 30. And he's not my boy toy."

"But you'd like him to be?"

I took a slug of Mimosa, tossing it back like I was doing

shots. Then my head dropped to my hands and I let out a groan.

"Oh my God, Becky! He's the hottest guy I've ever met. Handsome, sexy, total brooding bad boy. But sweet, too. How can an ex-thief be sweet? And I don't even know if he's an ex-thief—not really. And when he looks at me, all dark and intense ... and I haven't had a boyfriend since Nathan. I haven't even had a date. And now my B.O.B. needs new batteries."

She choked on her drink then burst out laughing.

"There's no harm in having a little down time thinking about doing the nasty with a hot felon. As long as that's all it is."

I sighed. Becky knew me too well.

"I like him."

She screwed her eyes shut.

"Oh glory, I was afraid of that. You're so predictable, El. You see something broken and you want to fix it. It's admirable in the right circumstances, but this isn't one of them."

"I know. I know you're right, but it's chemistry, or magnetism, or pheromones, or..."

"Lust?"

I looked down at the drink in my hands.

"Honey, the guy is hot and off-limits and the original bad boy. Of course you're lusting after him. Just promise me that you won't do anything stupid."

"As if!" I huffed.

"Hmm, well, tell me this. If he was paroled tomorrow, would you date him? Introduce him to me? To the rest of your friends? Would you take him home to meet your parents? Can you honestly see a future with an ex-con?"

I shook my head.

"I'm his teacher. Nothing is going to happen."

But the truth was, it already had. I was falling for Prisoner 97813. It was reckless and stupid, maybe even dangerous.

And I couldn't stop myself.

Garrett

I was going crazy. I didn't think I could take another lesson of sitting so close to her, smelling the warm scent of her skin and not being able to touch her. Sitting there so hard that my dick was ready to leap out of my pants every time I breathed. And when she moved, the warmth of her body heating the air between us, I had to press the palms of my hands onto the sharp corner of my desk to distract myself. I'd considered quitting the class, just to get away from the chaos of feelings that could never be returned.

It was haunting, taunting, teasing me. I couldn't rest, couldn't sleep, couldn't damn well think!

I had to know the truth. I had to know if everything I was feeling was just an illusion, just inside my head.

Hudson was watching me pace up and down our 8 x 6 foot cell.

"Jesus, Garrett! You're giving me a fucking stress headache!"

I ignored him, and carried on pacing, needing to release the restless, zinging energy born of frustration and uncertainty.

"Look, man, if we was on the outside, you'd tap that sweet ass and be over it, right?"

I shrugged. I didn't think Ella Newsome was the kind of woman a man got over, but there was no point saying that to Hudson.

"Well, we're in here, so you can't—although you've been jerking off so much, I think *I'm* gonna go blind."

"And your fucking point?" I snarled.

"You gotta find out if she's really into you."

I laughed viciously.

"You're a fucking genius. Sure, I'll just go up to her in front of Wilson, or maybe the whole class, and ask her if she's into felons, and if she thinks I look good in orange. Fuck me!"

"That's exactly what you do," Hudson said, grinning like an idiot. "And before you go PMSing on me, you do it at the end of the lesson after everyone has left. I'll get into it with that prick Fisher in the corridor—it'll be my extreme fucking pleasure. Wilson will come outside to break it up, and you'll have about ten or fifteen seconds to find out if she's dick-happy for you."

I thought about it. The idea has possibilities, except...

"You'll end up in solitary for that. Loss of privileges for a month."

He shrugged.

"Nah. Wilson isn't that much of an asshole, but if I do— whatever. It's gotta be better than watching you being a sad little bitch."

I thought about it. I thought of all the reasons why it was a bad idea, and what it could mean for Hudson—or for Ella—if we were caught. I didn't care what happened to me —I hadn't for a long time now. But a kernel of hope had been planted, and I was having a hard time uprooting it.

If she blew me off, fine. I'd just fantasize about her and that would be it. The sweetest, most caring woman I'd ever met. But if, if she gave me some sort of acknowledgement...

After that, my thoughts went blank. It seemed so impossible, I couldn't imagine anything. Nada. My chest burned with horror that there might be nothing out there for me in the world. Just a life of struggling with my past, always labeled an ex-con. Mistrusted and despised. A barely literate felon with a shady history. A dead-end life.

I must be crazy if I thought Ella would want someone like me. Fuck, she'd have to be nuts herself.

I turned to Hudson.

"Let's do it."

Ella

There was a weird energy in the class today. The students seemed restless, like wild animals trapped in a cage, and I was reminded more than usual that they weren't here of their own free will.

I was very happy to stay behind my desk and let the men come to me, and I was very glad to have Officer Wilson's calm presence beside me.

Garrett didn't look at me once, keeping his eyes on the textbook in his hands.

The man who sat next to him, Hudson, kept looking across at another prisoner and smirking. And that guy, Fisher, was an irritation—one of the few men who still made inappropriate comments about me.

I didn't know what was going on, but it felt like a storm was brewing.

Despite my misgivings, the class passed without incident. I handed out the homework assignments and dismissed them.

They filed out quietly, and I was happy to hear several of them discussing the class. I noticed that Garrett was hanging back, and my foolish heart lurched at the thought he wanted to talk to me.

Suddenly, there were raised voices and the sounds of fists meeting flesh outside the classroom, and Officer Wilson rushed out.

Leaving me alone with Garrett.

He stood up quickly, and in five long strides, he pushed the classroom door shut and was at my side.

"Ella," he whispered, his face filled with hope and anguish.

He swallowed several times, looking toward the door and back at me.

"Ella, I have to know. Am I feeling this alone?" and he gestured between our bodies. "Tell me I'm a fucking idiot and I'll leave you alone, I promise. But I have to know—I'm going crazy with ... with hope."

I was shocked, stunned to my core. Joy burned fiercely, a comet scorching across my heart. Burning too hot to be touched or tamed.

"You're not alone," I stammered. "I feel it, too. I..."

But whatever words I might have said were lost.

Garrett pulled me toward him, his rough hands gripping my wrist and waist. My chest collided with his, my softness giving in to his hardness.

I thought his mouth would crash down on mine, assaulting me. Instead, he waited, his eyes questioning, his lips reluctant, until I freed my hands and tangled my fingers in his unruly hair, pulling his head lower so I could take what I needed, what I'd longed for.

I was the one assaulting him, hot and urgent, my body burning fiercely, all the truths I thought I knew about myself lost in the erotic madness of our kiss.

A low, feral moan rolled up from his chest, and I tasted his desire and urgency as his tongue swept into my mouth. I could hear his breathing, harsh in his chest, his eyes wild and dilated, and they were staring at me as if they could burn a path into my soul.

He pulled me tighter, forcing his leg between my thighs, showing me the way I affected him, solid and thick.

An alarm blaring jerked us apart, and Garrett peered through the window in the classroom door.

When he turned to look at me again, there was a new tension in his jaw.

"They're going to riot," he said sharply. "We have to get out of here. Do you trust me?"

Trust. Such a small word with such a big meaning. Could I trust a convicted felon? Could I? Dare I trust a man whose simple words stole my heart from the very first moment he'd shown me his true self? Foolish, foolish heart.

"Yes, I trust you."

A surprised smile flashed across his face, then he shook his head.

"We have to get out of here. It's not safe for you."

Panic shot through me, but then Garrett grabbed my hand and I felt instantly soothed.

He peered around the door, paused, then squeezed my fingers without looking at me.

"Get ready to run, Ella."

I took a deep breath, and then we were racing along the brightly lit corridor, the alarm even louder, almost drowning out the pounding of our footsteps.

Garrett dragged me along with him, urging me to go faster. I felt his own panic as he tried door after door, but all were locked. The sound of rioting seemed to follow us, and I thought I could smell smoke.

Then we ran out of corridor, and Garrett swore loudly, his eyes darting wildly. He dropped my hand and kicked at the nearest door, smashing it repeatedly until I was sure either the door or his leg would shatter.

Finally, as sweat poured down Garrett's face, the door's weak lock screeched and broke, and he fell into a large storage closet.

"In here!" he hissed, his face contorting with pain as his hand reached out to mine.

I followed him without thinking, needing him near to feel safe.

As soon as I was inside, he wedged the door shut, and we sat with our backs against the wall, breathless. Only a faint illumination came through the cracks around the door frame until my eyes adjusted to the darkness.

Garrett was watching me warily.

"Are you okay?"

A small, hysterical laugh bubbled out of me.

"Am I? I don't know! Are you okay?"

"Yeah."

So much emotion in that one word. I felt his longing, shared it.

My hands cupped his face, using the darkness as permission to explore him slowly. His eyelids drooped and he breathed in a shaky breath.

"Ella, I don't..."

"Shh," I whispered, pressing my lips against the soft skin of his neck, breathing in the faint scent of plain soap and sweat.

His body shuddered as my fingers explored further, adrenaline and shock making me bold. We'd been gifted this one chance and I wasn't going to waste it.

I'd imagined that hard body so many times, imagined the layer of solid muscle and silky skin that overlaid a tall, lean bone structure. My impatient fingers pushed under his prison uniform, discovering a trail of coarse hair that led from his chest to the waistband of his pants.

My impulsive fingers drifted lower, and I felt the groan in his chest as I closed my hand around his hot, heated shaft.

"Ellaaaa!" he moaned my name with reverence, a plea.

I squeezed, not gentle, and the movement broke him.

He rolled to his knees, pressing his body above mine, forcing me to the floor.

"If you don't want this, for fuck's sake, stop me now, because once I start..."

I shut off his words with an impatient, claiming kiss, that told him, showed him, exactly what I wanted. A harsh growl rolled up his throat, and his body pressed harder on mine, one hand squeezing my breast, pinching the nipple harshly.

I wanted more. Sweet Garrett, gentle Garrett, the man with those dark, questioning eyes, the man who watched me and wanted me—and now I wanted the whole man.

I pushed his hands away and pulled my ugly t-shirt upward, but within a heartbeat, he'd ripped it over my head, unsnapping my bra with one hand, his tongue plunging between my breasts as he sucked and licked and bit and feasted.

We fought to rid ourselves of clothes as fast as possible in the cramped, dark, smelly storeroom, bleach and dirt burning my nostrils.

I couldn't get my slacks over my sneakers, the fabric caught below my knees. I hissed with frustration.

Garrett was quicker, kicking his loose pants over his shoes, his utilitarian boxers gone in a second.

Those long, beautiful fingers, those artist's hands, pressed against my core, gathering my wetness. I was shocked and aroused when he thrust his fingers into his mouth, his eyes rolling back in his head as he tasted me.

The alarm wailed louder, shrieking *DANGER! DANGER!* and the shouting grew closer.

"Garrett!" I whispered, my voice shaking with fear and desire.

"God, I want to make love to you," he grunted, "but we've got to be quick. Say yes to me, Ella. Say it now!"

"Yes!" I gasped.

Without asking permission again, he gripped my waist and tossed me to my hands and knees. I whimpered softly, his strength and possessiveness soothing the bruises that were sure to be visible on my knees by morning.

I felt the moist, blunt tip of his erection positioned at my entrance, and a second later he was inside me. No condom, no barrier, no safety net.

I nearly screamed as I felt like I'd been split in half, but his rough hand clamped over my mouth. I pushed my ass backward, taking more of him, feeling the wild slapping of his balls against me as we rutted in the dark, two animals fucking away our fear.

His hand moved from my mouth, and he rubbed my clit furiously, skill gone, speed essential.

My whole body shuddered as his chest pressed over my back. His hot breath seethed into my skin as he bit my shoulder, my neck, and when he came suddenly, his lips kissed away the pain.

For a second, we gasped together, our breaths loud in the small space. And then he pulled out and I felt the warm stream of his cum, pool then drip down my leg. I didn't even have time to wipe him from my skin when the alarm cut out ominously. I pulled up my pants, rooting around in the dark for my bra and shirt.

"Ella?"

I don't know what he would have said to me. I never found out.

Because the door was yanked open.

Officer Wilson stood there, baton in hand, his stance defensive as his suspicious eyes flicked between us.

"Garrett? Miss Newsome?"

My face burned like a beacon of dishonesty, and I gasped for breath, a dying fish.

"Is it safe?" I asked hoarsely.

His suspicion receded an inch.

"All taken care of," he replied, his frown directed at Garrett. "Nothing to worry about. Are you sure you're okay?"

"I was scared," I lied, my eyelashes fluttering as more untruths fell from my mouth. "Garrett ... so I'd be ... safe."

The biggest lie. Garrett was very far from being safe. He was the most dangerous man I'd ever met, because I'd given him the power to reduce me to ashes. My body surged again, wanting him, wanting more.

I gripped the wall behind me, and when Wilson's worried face turned toward me, he couldn't see the anxious possession in Garrett's eyes.

"I'm fine," I lied. "All good here. Nothing happened."

Garrett stood slowly, his back pressed against the wall, his fists slammed against his side as his eyes shot to mine.

"Yeah, nothing at all."

CHAPTER SIX

GARRETT

I thought my heart would explode.

I'd never been ripped apart by a kiss, by fucking; woken, raised from the dead, killed and risen again. I don't know who the hell I was, but it wasn't Prisoner 97813 anymore.

She let me kiss her, use her like a whore on her knees, and she moaned my name.

I didn't believe in miracles. I never had. But now ... Ella Newsome had wanted me. I tasted it in her kiss, saw it in her eyes, felt it in her body as she shuddered beneath me, my cock inside her. *She'd wanted me, come for me.*

I was too undone to feel joy, too scared of the overwhelming, overpowering sensations still vibrating through my body.

Wilson knew. It was obvious what had happened, even though he hadn't seen anything directly. And that was a problem.

I was escorted back to my cell, seeing everywhere the bloodied, bruised faces of other prisoners, surprised but pleased that Hudson was on his bunk waiting for me. Hardly the worse for wear, except for a swollen eye, slowing turning purple.

He grinned and swung down from his bunk, slouching next to me on my hard mattress.

"I don't need to ask, man. You look like you've had one o' them epiphanies, like in the Bible. Congratulations. You got laid in prison by our hot teacher. You're officially a legend. Now what you going to do next?"

I shook my head, words tied around my tongue.

Before I could find my balance, Wilson was standing at the door with Reynolds.

"You need to come with us, Garrett."

Reynolds stroked his right hand over his baton as he leered at me.

"I always knew you were scum."

Ella

It was a mistake.

In a lifetime of bad choices, this had to be the worst. And that included the time I let Jason Waters talk me into sharing a blunt and losing my virginity to him in the back of his father's truck. Even when I found out that he'd given me crabs.

This was worse.

I stared up at the barbed wire and tall searchlights that fringed the entrance to Nottoway Correctional Center. Even the bland, blue sky seemed grayer here, heavier, ill at ease.

Adrenaline was pumping, and my fight or flight response was kicking in: I wanted to run. Fast.

When I put my car into drive, my hands were still shaking...

I couldn't believe I'd taken such a stupid risk—not just for me, but for Garrett, too.

It was sheer, dumb luck that we hadn't been caught. Five seconds sooner, and Wilson would have found us.

I closed my eyes, the heat of Garrett still inside me. *I must be insane.*

My choices rolled out before me: bleak, gray.

I could quit my job, or I could dismiss Garrett from the class. What I couldn't do was continue to teach him. Not after this.

But he'd done nothing wrong. He'd asked my *permission.* I was the one at fault. And it wasn't fair for him to lose the chance of working for his GED or even losing his parole because of me.

I wasn't sure that my bank would think much of me being unemployed, and I knew I couldn't make more than two mortgage payments without a job.

I wondered how easy it would be to get work as a substitute teacher. It certainly wouldn't pay as well as teaching in a prison.

God, I was a mess, and it was my own stupid fault. Was it like Becky said, that getting involved with a convict would drag me down?

Sick with self-inflicted misery, I sat in my apartment, a bottle of wine in front of me. I gulped down two glasses without pausing.

Then to rub salt into gaping wounds, I pulled out the men's latest assignments, searching until I found Garrett's.

> *Our assignment is to say why the caracter in* Hunger *does the things he does. It's because he's starving, and a man will do pretty much anything if he's desperet for something to eat.*
>
> *I was born in McDowell County, WV. It's not a*

city or anything, but it's still like Christiana where the story is set. But if you went there you'd see broken windows on shuttered businesses and homes crumbling into dirt. Nothing new has been built in years, decades may be.

My father died of an overdose in 2007, and my mama is gone. My neighbors lived on disability payments.

John F. Kennedy came here in 1960 and his first order as President was to give us the food stamp program. When President Lyndon B. Johnson came four years later, we got federal programs like Medicare, Medicaid, and free school lunches.

Old folk say those was good times because now the mines are closed and there are no jobs. If you've gotten a roof over your head, your probably in prison, like me.

So I know what that guy in Hunger *went through. People say he's crazy, but when you're starving, stealing a car isn't crazy, it's survival.*

PS I've got a big question to ask you and I know I have no right. But I'm going to ask it anyway, because I haven't felt like a man in a long time, but thats how you make me feel. So even if this is goodby, I want to thank you first.

Sinceerly,
Dane Garrett, Prisoner 97813

I laid the paper down, tears blurring my vision and dripping onto the cheap paper with its looping, penciled scrawl.

He'd planned today, I saw that now. His friend, Hudson,

had started the riot just to give him a chance to ask me his 'big question'. It had turned into so much more than that.

So much more.

I'd resign tomorrow, because a man like Garrett deserved a chance to make something of his life. He needed to take his GED, but I wasn't the teacher for him. Not anymore.

I couldn't be in a class with him and not show everyone what he meant to me. We'd stepped over the line and there was no going back. For either of us.

I didn't sleep that night.

Although I'd made my decision, I wasn't certain what the consequences would be of a sudden resignation. I could quite possibly be putting my whole career in jeopardy.

My intention was to lie, and say that I found the prison system too frightening. After yesterday's near riot, they were sure to believe me. It wasn't even untrue.

I dressed carefully the next morning, flouting the rules by wearing makeup, applying a small amount of concealer under my eyes to hide the dark circles.

As I drove up to the visitors' parking lot, my palms began to sweat, feeling slick as I held the steering wheel.

And as I submitted to the usual body search, I felt guilt in every stuttering breath.

But when it came to resign my job, the words died in my throat.

Because Garrett was leaving—already awaiting transfer to another prison.

Because of me.

I saw it in Wilson's frown. And I saw it Reynolds's repugnant grin.

They knew.

And when I told them I was sick and had to go to the

bathroom, I locked myself inside and cried. Tears of guilt and hurt and frustration.

And then I went to my classroom and taught the rest of my students to the best of my ability, because they deserved that chance.

Hudson didn't speak a word to me. And for that, I was grateful.

CHAPTER SEVEN

GARRETT

Fall was fading, and the air was crisper and colder. But my heart was ice, and it was Winter every day.

Another prison, but just the same.

The same walls, the same cells, the same concrete in every direction that you looked. The same tiny patch of sky overhead—a rectangle of blue that mocked me every day.

At Thanksgiving we got turkey.

At Christmas we got beef.

At New Year we got ham.

But it all tasted like dust to me.

They wouldn't let me write her, because you can't send letters to staff. That's what they told me. I don't know if it's true. So I wrote to Hudson instead. He probably got a big laugh out of that, me sending him a letter.

Six weeks later, he wrote back. He said it would have been sooner, but he'd gotten into it with Fisher again, and had spent a week in solitary and a month without privileges —like getting mail.

Ella still taught at Nottoway. I was pleased about that. I was afraid she'd gotten canned.

I told Hudson that if he got the chance he should tell her not to write me. I didn't even know if she was thinking that, but she'd dodged one bullet because of me, and I didn't want her in the firing line again.

I missed her.

I missed her lessons. I missed our conversations. I missed the way she looked at me, like I wasn't filth, like I was worth something. I dreamed about the way she'd kissed me, the way her body had pressed against mine.

And in the long, bitter nights, when the screams and moans of other prisoners echoed in the air, I'd take my swollen dick in my hand, the veins standing out on the stiff column of flesh, and I'd imagine it was her small hand stroking the crown, tempting, teasing, tasting. And I'd come on my stomach with a quiet sigh, because it was never enough.

And the lonely ache felt as if someone had ripped off a limb and forgotten to tell me. I hurt all the time, walking with my shoulders slumped like some old man. At first, the other sinners thought they could make me their bitch because I was so quiet, my mind always elsewhere. After I'd proved that I wasn't a new fish, they left me alone pretty much.

I was alone in a prison that suffered from overcrowding.

I sent one more letter to Hudson, giving him the time and date of my parole, and a promise that when he got out, if I had a place to stay by then, he could share it with me— even though felons are supposed to stay away from other felons.

He didn't write back.

~

It was Tuesday, February 7, and there was snow on the ground, making the world look fresh and new. I wasn't the man who'd been put away five years ago, but I wasn't fresh and new either.

I was wearing the same clothes that I'd been arrested in, my jeans still baggy, but my t-shirt tighter than it had been because I'd bulked up some in prison. All those reps with Hudson, I guess.

I shivered, because I'd been picked up in the summer so right now I didn't have a coat or even a sweater. Leaving prison was like being reborn, they said. You came into the world exactly as you left it. Big fucking joke.

My parole officer had given me the address of the halfway house, a bus ticket, and $63 plus some change that I'd earned in prison. Five years wages—the wages of sin, my grandma would have said.

I was free, but I didn't think that made me a rich man. And being free wasn't like I imagined or hoped. It was easier inside because it was familiar. No wonder so many of us went back again and again.

I shoved my hands deep in my pockets, shoulders hunched from cold, eyes squinting as the snow glinted in the sun.

I decided against freezing my ass off at the bus stop, so I started to walk, enjoying the way my footsteps crunched in the fresh snow, awed by the ice crystals clinging to the bare branches of trees, watching my breath frost in the frigid air.

Man, it was cold.

I shivered, wondering how long it would take me to get to the halfway house and claim my shitty room that was probably the same size as my old cell, just not as homey.

But as a car pulled up beside me, and the window rolled down, I was instantly wary.

"Garrett!"

I stared, certain I was having an out-of-body experience. And I didn't move.

"It's me ... Ella ... from Nottoway."

As if I could forget.

This was every dream, every fantasy, every stupid hope rolled up into this moment, this woman. And it was wrong. All wrong. *She shouldn't be here.*

My body unlocked, and I took a step forward. She blinked rapidly, her expression fearful and hopeful.

Her hair had grown and brushed her shoulders, thick and shiny. And she was wearing makeup, her eyes sultry, her lips redder. I breathed in deeply, the familiar scent lighting fires under my skin.

"Ella."

I must have sounded as stupid as I looked, because she gave a soft smile.

"Yes, it's me. Oh my gosh! I was so afraid that I'd missed you! Stupid traffic! How are you?"

I stared at her silently, watching as she frowned and pressed her lips into a flat line at my silence.

"Can I ... give you a ride somewhere? You must be freezing."

I was still staring.

"Hudson told you?"

She nodded, her cheeks pink.

"I've been arguing with myself ever since ... but here I am. If you want me?"

Did a drowning man want to breathe? But just to be sure...

"You want to give me a ride? You okay being seen with a con?"

"An ex-con," she said softly. "Yes, I am."

I pulled open the door and slid into the small seat,

sighing as warmth from the car's heaters brushed my bare arms.

"Don't you have a coat? Sorry, stupid question. If you had a coat, you'd be wearing it."

She threw me an anguished glance as I studied a loose thread in the knee of my jeans.

Our second time alone together, and things had never been more awkward.

"Thanks for stopping by."

She bit her lip.

"Sure. Where can I take you?"

I pulled out the address of the halfway house, and she programmed it into her GPS.

We rode in silence, the tension spiraling almost out of control. Almost. Because anything that happened had to come from her. Yeah, she was here now, but I needed to know if this was just guilt or pity. It hurt too much to hope for something else. And besides, I didn't deserve it. So I stayed silent.

Finally, she pulled up at the curb of a crumbling townhouse, the cracked paving slabs that made up the tiny yard filled with weeds.

I didn't want to get out of the car, but she wasn't giving me anything. Nothing.

I turned to open the door, taking one last look at her beautiful face.

"Thanks for the ride."

Ella

The car journey was so stressful, my anxiety levels went shooting upwards. There was no desk between us, no guard watching over us, no noise of riot masking our moans as we fucked in the dark. Garrett was here, filling the car with his large body, a scent of soap and man. His face was pinched with cold, but even as the warmth from my car's heater blew across him, he still wouldn't look at me.

My pulse was racing and I felt sure he must hear my heart pounding. My body reacted as if just seconds had passed since he'd been inside me, not four, long, lonely months.

But he was so closed and withdrawn—more like the man I'd met on my first day at Nottoway, rather than the one who'd kissed me like he needed it more than breathing, fucked me like the world was ending.

And now we were parked outside the ugly, soulless halfway house in a rundown part of the city. It wasn't one of the more modern, specially designed buildings that I'd read about. Instead, it was an old townhouse, once adapted into apartments and now used to house and rehabilitate men who'd just left prison.

His hand fastened around the door handle, and he didn't look at me as he spoke.

"Thanks for the ride."

His voice was low and harsh, and I didn't know what it meant.

"Wait!"

His hand tightened on the door handle, but his dark, shuttered eyes slid to mine.

"Um ... I..."

He sighed and looked away.

"It's okay, Ella. You were my teacher and I was your student. I don't expect anything from you."

And there it was. A man who'd been let down so many times, he expected to be rejected at every turn as if there was no alternative.

"Garrett, I mean, Dane ... I don't want this to be

goodbye. I think ... I think we have something. Something special."

His cold eyes stared at me, and he didn't speak.

"If it's all in my head, tell me, please. If you just wanted to ... fuck a teacher, you'd have told everyone, been the big man. But you didn't. So I think ... I think..."

I swear I could see the ice melting in his eyes.

And he didn't need to speak.

He reached toward me, tentatively taking a lock of my hair between his fingers and rubbing it, feeling the texture. Then he tucked it behind my ear and leaned closer.

His lips pressed softly against mine, and I sank forward into the safe circle of his arms.

Yes, this was where I wanted to be. And soon, not today, but soon, we'd visit the ocean. We'd stand on the beach, staring out at the Atlantic, at all that space, the wide horizon with all its possibilities. And we'd watch the sun sink and the long shadows stretch across the sand. And we'd plan our future.

My words whispered against his neck.

"I was your teacher, but you're the one who taught me about myself, about who I could be."

He straightened up, his hands stroking through my hair.

"You are the most amazing person I've ever met. You're good and kind and smart and so damn beautiful." His hands dropped to his lap. "And I'll never forget you."

Before I could say another word, he opened the door and strode toward the halfway house.

CHAPTER EIGHT

GARRETT

Walking away from her was the hardest thing I'd ever done. And the best.

Life had taught me that if you don't make yourself number one, no one else will. Until I'd met Ella. She'd put her energy and strength into helping a bunch of loser jailbirds, and she never once looked down on any of us. Not even the assholes like Fisher.

She'd taught us writing and shit that would help us pass our GEDs, but it was *her*; the way she talked and smiled, the way she treated us as equals—that was the real lesson. There are people in the world who give a shit; there are people who will put others before themselves.

Seeing her in that little car of hers the day I was released ... yeah, that nearly broke me.

But if she stayed with me, I'd bring her down to my level: in the gutter, among the garbage.

And that's why I had to walk away from her.

As I rang the bell on the door of the halfway house, I

refused to look behind me. I knew she was still parked at the curb, watching.

Drive away, damn you!

A tall dude with a salt and pepper beard and glasses opened the door, glancing over my shoulder then fixing his pale eyes on me.

"Garrett, right?"

"Yes, sir."

"The name's Clyde. Come on in. That your ride out there?"

I hesitated before giving a curt nod.

"She coming in?"

I shook my head.

He glanced at Ella once more, then closed the door behind me.

"Okay, son. This will be your home for the next three months. You'll get your own room, three meals a day, mandatory counseling, and we'll help you find work. Curfew is 11PM: miss it, and you'll be in violation of your parole which means you'll finish the rest of your sentence in prison. Any guests have to be on an approved list, and there are no overnight stays. You won't drink alcohol or take drugs, and there'll be weekly testing to make sure you stay clean. Your room can be searched at any time." He paused. "I'm told that you've been studying for your GED?"

"I was."

"We'll get you signed up for night school. You got any belongings with you? Anything going to be sent on to you?"

I shook my head.

"No? Well, we have a stock of clothes from the Salvation Army that might fit you. You got any questions?"

"No, sir."

He turned and led me into the dimly-lit hallway, his winter boots loud on the tattered linoleum.

He called over his shoulder, "Welcome to Beacon House."

Ella

I watched him walk away, but I didn't follow. I was so shocked, I didn't know what to do. He'd been ice cold, then burning hot, then shuttered, and finally his eyes had closed as if it was too painful to look at me.

So I went home, ran a hot bath, my tears mingling with the soapy water.

When I'd cried myself out and watched my skin wrinkle like a prune, I climbed sluggishly from the tepid water, lethargic and empty.

My thick terrycloth robe was comforting, and I wrapped it around me tightly as I curled up on the sofa, bewildered and unsure as shadows crept across the bare ceiling.

Four months, I'd imagined every possible outcome of Garrett's release day. The date had been marked on my calendar ever since Hudson had written it at the end of an essay. But it turned out that I was wrong, because none of my imaginings had ended with Dane Garrett walking away.

I wished I could talk to Becky, but I couldn't. As far as she knew, Dane had been transferred for reasons unknown. She'd commiserated on me missing my 'hottie-con' to ogle. She didn't know what had happened that day, or that his transfer was my fault. And she had no clue that I still thought about him every day and dreamed about him every night. I certainly hadn't told her that I was planning to meet him the day he was released.

Her words echoed in my brain: *"If he was paroled tomorrow, would you date him? Introduce him to your friends?*

Would you take him home to meet your parents? Can you honestly see a future with an ex-con?"

I'd denied it at the time, but now it seemed the answer to those questions was simply *yes*.

My friends wouldn't understand, and my parents would be horrified. And I wasn't completely naïve—I knew how hard it was for people who'd been in prison to make it on the outside. I desperately wanted Dane to succeed, and I *hated* that he'd never gotten to take his GED because of me. I owed it to him as well as myself to try again.

So, I went over every word, every action, every look that he'd given me, replaying it all in my mind.

From this, I drew two conclusions: first, Dane didn't want to say goodbye—something was making him act that way; and second, I was *not* going to let him go without a fight.

I had work to do.

Garrett

I flattened the palm of my hand against the cold pane of glass and stared out.

There were no bars on this window, and I could see snow laying thickly outside, the sidewalks covered in slush. Heavy clouds were half hidden by neighboring buildings and the world seemed washed with gray.

I looked around my tiny room, taking in the narrow bed, empty bookshelf, and hooks on the wall to hang my clothes.

I'd been looking forward to this day for five long years: 1,825 miserable fucking days, 43,801 torturous hours. I should be happy, I should be fucking delirious, but instead, I felt turned inside out and empty.

I dreamed about her, and every waking moment was

filled with silent questions. *Where are you? What are you doing right now? Are you happy, Ella?*

I kept busy, in the way people who are afraid to think fill their hours with *doing*. I'd attended two of the mandatory group counseling sessions, listening to some dickhead tell me to remember to wipe my ass after shitting because that would make me more of a model citizen. The other ex-cons dozed off during these fun little lectures.

I exercised in my cell-like room, pushups and crunches until I vomited; I circled every job in the newspaper, the words *no experience necessary* drawing my attention like a beacon. There weren't many. I waited in line to get my turn at one of the two computers, searching job sites. I filled in job applications, typing with one finger:

Qualifications. *Answer: none.*

Recent employment. *Answer: none.*

Reason for leaving last job. *Answer: Grand Theft Auto.*

Clyde wasn't so bad, doing what he said he'd do and fixing me up with night school so I could at least get my high school equivalency. On my third day, he said he had a lead on a job for me, too. And if everything went well, I'd be fulfilling my lifelong ambition to say, "You want fries with that?"

But work was work, and it would feel good to have money in my wallet.

Ella. No, don't think about her.

"Garrett, you there?"

Clyde knocked on my door, then opened it and peered inside.

"How you doing?"

I shrugged.

"Well, slap a smile on your face and get your ass over to East Broad Street. You're interviewing with the manger,

Ms. Carter." His hard expression softened fractionally. "She's expecting you."

I'd never had a job interview before, never held down regular work. I'd helped out in a couple of auto repair shops, being paid off the books, but that had all been by knowing a guy who knew a guy. I'd been in juvie, then a few years of living on the wire, then done my stint in stir.

All that must have shown on my face because Clyde clapped a meaty hand on my shoulder and looked me in the eye.

"She knows you're an ex-con, son, and she's willing to give you a chance. Just be truthful and polite."

I shrugged into my secondhand coat, and pulled a tattered beanie over my too-long hair, then pocketed the bus fare that Clyde gave me, and squinted at the street map.

The burger bar was brightly-lit and full of people. The neon glare made my eyes hurt and the crowd made me edgy.

I pushed open the door, the warm air scented with grease blowing across my face. My eyes skated anxiously over the customers and the servers working the counter. Unsure what to do, I joined a line.

When my turn came, the bored blonde blinked up at me, not even bothering to smile.

"How may I help you today?"

I don't really want to help you. Go away. Leave me alone. I serve fries in my sleep.

"I've come for a job, um, about working here?"

My words sounded uncertain, tumbling awkwardly from my mouth.

"You need Ms. Carter. She expectin' you?"

"Yes, ma'am."

Unexpectedly, she giggled.

" 'Ma'am?' Oh wow, you're a hoot!" Then she pointed over her shoulder at a door that said 'Staff Only'. "Go on through."

I nodded and walked away, only thinking after that I should have thanked her.

My palms began to sweat. How could I be normal when I'd never known what that meant?

At my cautious knock, the door opened.

"I'm Garrett. Um, Dane. I was sent..."

"Oh yeah, right. Come on in."

A tired-looking woman with a heavily pregnant belly waved me into the tiny cubicle and pointed at a folding chair.

"So, Dane ... any customer service experience?"

"No, ma'am."

"Any catering experience?"

"I worked in the kitchens when I was ... I've done some kitchen work."

She looked up, sucking her teeth thoughtfully.

"I'll be frank with you. I'm doing this because Clyde did my cousin a favor when he came out of prison. I'll give you a week's trial. Only the district manager knows about you— none of the staff here, and I'd like to keep it that way. Word gets out that I've got an ex-con working here and next thing you know things go missing, the till ends up short..."

My face got hot and I had to force myself to stay sitting.

She held up a hand.

"I'm just saying that some people would see it as an opportunity to cover their own tracks, you feel me? I got a few staff I know and trust, but a lot of short-timers, too. And customers can be just as tricky. They say they give you a twenty, but they only give you a ten. You've got to be careful. So you being an ex-con stays between you and me. Got it?"

"Yes, ma'am."

"Hmm. Anything you good at, Dane?"

Yeah, fucking up my life.

"I can fix car engines."

"Can you now? Well, how you think you'd get on with our second deep fryer? I phoned for an repairman three weeks ago and ain't seen sign of one yet."

"I can try."

She smiled for the first time.

"Keep that attitude and you and me gonna get on just fine."

Ella

The manager at the halfway house wouldn't tell me anything about Dane. But then his eyes narrowed, flitting to my Mini Cooper.

"You gave Garrett a ride the day he arrived."

"That was me!"

He scratched his beard thoughtfully.

"Wife? Sister?"

I shook my head.

"Friend," I said weakly.

He nodded slowly.

"Who should I say dropped by?"

"Ella."

"Any message, Ella?"

"Tell him..." I lifted my chin. "Tell him I can hear the birds sing, too. And that I'll be waiting."

His smile was kind.

"I'll tell him."

❧

I came by every day after I'd finished at Nottoway, leaving one prison for Dane's self-imposed banishment, but he was never there. On the fourth day, Clyde took pity on me.

"He's at work, Ella. I shouldn't really be telling you this ... but he gets off at 10PM. If you decide to wait for him, I can't stop you."

I couldn't help flinging my arms around his neck, thanking him over and over, wringing an embarrassed chuckle from him as he awkwardly patted my back.

"Keep your car doors locked."

I came back that evening on the dot of ten. Since I didn't know how far away Dane worked, waiting was agonizing. And a little creepy, sitting alone in the dark.

Finally, after I'd been waiting the better part of an hour, I saw him. Despite the heavy overcoat obscuring his body, and the woolen hat covering his hair, I recognized him immediately. Even the loping stride was new, but my body warmed instinctively, drawn to its other half.

I stumbled out of the car, adrenaline surging through me.

"Dane! Dane, wait!"

He glanced both ways along the street before he strode over to me, gripping the top of the car door as I stood in the gutter staring up at him.

"What are you doing here, Ella? I told you..."

"I know what you told me, but I'm not letting you go like that. Please."

I trembled from cold and longing, desperate to touch him.

He sighed with frustration, then gestured for me to get back in the car. When he slid into the passenger seat next to me, the car was filled with the pungent smell of chicken fat.

"You shouldn't be here."

I took a deep breath, ignoring the unpleasant aroma of fried food.

"I had to come."

"You need to leave."

I reached out for his cold hand, wrapping it in my smaller ones.

"I miss your voice, I miss your smile. I miss the way you run your fingers through your hair when you're upset or annoyed. I miss the way the left hand side of your mouth lifts when you're trying not to smile. I miss your letters. I miss reading about your hopes and dreams. You're finally free, Dane Garrett, and the only thing keeping us apart is you. I miss you."

He shook his head slowly and closed his eyes, pulling his hand away. When he spoke, he wouldn't look at me.

"You're wrong. I'm not free. I have a curfew every night. If I miss it, I'll be sent back. I can't have a beer, or I'll be sent back. I can't live where I want, or do a job I want. Right now, I'm stinking up your car because the only job I can get comes with a lifetime supply of onion rings."

"It's an honest day's work, Dane. There's no shame in that."

He turned to stare at me.

"I'm no good for you."

His voice was sharp, attacking, angry words.

"I decide who's good for me," I shot back, matching his rising fury. "No one else—just me. And I happen to think that a kind, thoughtful, caring man with gentle hands will suit me fine."

"Goddammit! Don't you ever listen?"

"Yes, I listen to my heart. And my heart wants you."

His rage ebbed like a turning tide, reluctant and slow.

He blinked, staring at me with puzzlement.

"Would you tell people? Would you tell your folks about how we met?"

"I'd tell them we met at work."

He snorted with amusement and irritation, then scrubbed his hands over his face.

"Prison is hard," he said softly. "But I know how it works. Out here..." and he gestured with one hand, leaving the sentence hanging.

"Then let me help you."

He shook his head.

"I'd only pull you down with me."

Finally, I was getting somewhere.

"Ah, I get it now."

"Get what?"

"Your noble act."

His jaw tightened and his eyes became small and mean.

"I'm not acting."

"Yes, you are. You're being all 'woe is me' because you think you're saving me from some faceless future. But you're not; you're being selfish."

"The fuck I am!"

"Yes, selfish! I have worried and waited for you. I watched you from a distance for three months before that. And now I'm waiting outside your apartment every night, freezing my ass off because you won't give me the time of day. I call that pretty damn selfish."

He stared at me with wide eyes, my storm of words soaking into him.

"Every night?"

"I didn't know you worked an evening shift until earlier today."

"You're too good for me..."

"According to my father, I'm too good for every man that doesn't walk on water," I growled, fixing him with a fierce scowl. "So perhaps I should just go be a nun. Is that your recommendation, too?"

"A fucking sexy nun," he muttered.

I laughed a little, and some of the tension left the air.

"Dane..." and I reached out to touch his cold cheek.

He leaned into my hand minutely, his lips opening.

"Dane, what's really keeping you away from me? What are you scared of?"

He moved away and sat up straighter.

"Failing." His eyes met mine. "I'm scared of failing ... of failing you."

"Oh, Dane, no..." I touched his cracked lips with my fingertip. "I've been so scared of failing *you!*"

CHAPTER NINE

ELLA

I was fifteen when I started dating, and I was one of those lucky kids whose parents said, "We just want you to be happy." Even when the boy I brought home had blue hair, a lip ring that he chewed on constantly, and played bass guitar—badly—in a thrash metal band. Although actually Kevin was rather sweet.

It was only when I dated in college that I realized, "We just want you to be happy" translated as, "We love you so much that we just want you to be happy, but preferably with a man who's a doctor and has a vacation home in the Hamptons."

By then, it was too late. I wanted to save a whale along with the starving poet I lived with for six months.

So that day, that evening, a night where the air seemed frozen, after Dane had kissed me with a hungry ferocity and steamed up the windows of my car to the point where someone might call a fire truck, I knew I had to break the news to my parents.

I called them the next evening and told Mom to put the phone on speaker.

"Mom, Dad, I've met someone special."

"Oh, darling! That's wonderful news! Tell us all about him."

My mother's happy voice rang across the airwaves. My father, more cautious asked, "Where did you meet him?"

"At work."

There was a short silence, a pregnant pause, you might say.

"He's a teacher in the prison service, like you?" Mom asked hopefully. "Or one of the corrections officers?"

"No. Dane was one of the students I taught."

A much longer silence followed, and I think Mom must have put her hand over the phone because their voices became muffled.

"I know this probably isn't the news you wanted to hear," I said calmly, "but you taught me to treat everyone with respect and that everyone deserves a second chance. Once you meet him, you'll see what an amazing man he is."

"Meet him?"

Mom's voice was confused, hesitant.

"Yes, he's out on parole. I'd like to bring him over for lunch on Sunday. If we're welcome."

"Oh, darling! Are you sure you're safe with him?"

Her voice trembled, words of warning ready to burst free.

"Yes," I answered simply. "I'm safe with him."

My father's voice was gruff.

"You'll always be welcome here, Ella. And we'll give your young man the benefit of the doubt."

They asked a few more questions, but tried hard to stay positive. I loved them so much for that.

Telling Becky was way worse.

We met in a coffee shop on Saturday afternoon, instead of our usual cocktail bar.

She grumbled about the change in location, but her eyes lit up when she saw the selection of muffins and cupcakes on offer.

Once we'd settled into the comfortable seats with our cakes and coffees, I faced my oldest friend.

"So, I have news."

She glanced at me sideways.

"Good news?"

"I think so, yes."

"Don't leave me hanging, El."

"Dane is out on parole and we're dating."

She paused, mid-chew, then swallowed the piece of cake she was eating and wiped her fingers on the paper napkin.

"What do you want me to say?"

Her voice was flat and dry, like a featureless desert, and my heart thumped with unease.

"That you're pleased I've met someone special, someone I care about. Someone I love."

Her grave expression softened into sadness.

"Have you really thought this through?"

I smiled and shook my head.

"Yes, no, I don't know. I've thought of nothing else for months. It won't be easy—prejudice is everywhere—but whenever I think of a future without him in it ... well, there's nothing but blankness. But with him, I see clearly: marriage, children, a life together."

Her lips tightened, and I saw disappointment and disapproval take root inside her.

"Ella, you can't throw your life away to try and save his."

Her words struck me in the heart, sharp and pointed.

"That's not what I'm doing."

"Isn't it? You asked me here so I could give you my opinion and I think this is a huge mistake that..."

"No, I asked you here because you're my best friend and I love you. I don't expect you to hold a parade, but at least give me the credit of understanding what I'm doing."

"My God, how can you? This will ruin your whole life!"

"I love him."

"Love doesn't pay bills! Love doesn't get you promotions at work! Love isn't enough—if that's what it really is, and not some bad boy crush, some long overdue teenage rebellion."

Painful, hurtful words.

"This isn't some childish crush."

"So you love your hottie-con. Based on what? A few meaningful glances across a crowded classroom? A few indiscreet notes passed during the lesson? Grow up, El!"

My face grew hot, and I had to remind myself that she didn't understand because I hadn't confided in her. How could I explain so she'd know that this was real? How could I tell her that our love started slowly, a single brick that laid a foundation? We'd been building our love gradually, moment by moment, letter by letter, brick by brick.

But before I could say anything, I glanced up to see Dane watching us, his expression hard and closed.

He walked towards us and I reached up to take his hand. He stepped closer, carrying his reluctance with him.

"Dane, this is my best friend Becky."

"Hello, Becky."

He held out his right hand for her to shake.

Her eyes raked him up and down, taking in his tired clothes and shabby shoes. But I saw that he'd shaved and had gotten a haircut. He looked handsome and serene, like a prince in disguise.

Becky touched the tips of her fingers to his, and shook hands curtly.

"Dane. So, I'm wondering: how badly are you going to fuck up Ella's life?"

"Becky!"

Anger and indignation warred with the years of friendship.

Garrett sat next to me, and although his words were for Becky, his gaze was fixed on mine.

"I'll try not to."

"Very reassuring," Becky sneered. "You must really have thought your luck had changed when you met Ella."

His dark eyes swung to hers.

"Yeah, I did."

She ignored him, turning to me.

"Ella, please think about what you're doing! Getting involved with him ... if the prison finds out, *which they will*, you'll be fired: professional misconduct. That will be on your record *forever*."

"They already know. That's why Dane was transferred."

Becky gaped at me.

"And they let you carry on teaching?"

"Yes. Well," I qualified, "they suspected an attachment between us. But now Dane is on parole, it's no one's business but ours."

"I can't believe you," she whispered, shaking her head. "What the hell are your parents going to say?"

"They've invited us for lunch tomorrow."

I saw her teetering on the brink of a decision, and I prayed that she'd accept this, prayed that she'd see the good in it.

She leaned closer, her eyes pleading with me.

"If this lasts, down the line there are jobs you won't get, because of him; there are people who won't let you teach their kids, because of him; there'll be restrictions and humiliations *all the way*."

"And there'll be other jobs, other chances, other people who won't care about the past."

"This is such a bad idea."

"Becky, just ... give him a chance! Give *us* a chance."

She shook her head again.

"I love you, Ella. When you come to your senses, I'll be there for you. This is a huge mistake, but it's your life. Don't say I didn't warn you."

She grabbed her coat and purse, striding from the coffee shop with her chin held high and tears in her eyes.

Her parting words felt like a curse.

Dane

"She'll come around."

Ella tried to sound confident, but her lips trembled. Her fingers wrapped around my arm and she held on tightly.

I didn't know what to say because every word Becky had said was true. A hot knife stabbed at my selfishness, but Ella only held me tighter.

"Don't listen to her," she said, even as Becky's words were tattooed into my brain. "She means well, but she's wrong."

I stared back impassively, and her face crumbled a little.

"She *is* wrong. Look how well you're doing already! You have a job and you're starting school next week. Dane, you should be proud of yourself because I am. I'm so proud of you."

She stroked my cheek, and I couldn't resist the warmth of her touch.

"You shaved," she whispered.

"I was trying to make a good impression," I laughed bitterly.

"I know. Thank you."

"It didn't help," I said, frowning at her.

She smiled sadly.

"Oh but it did."

I grunted in disagreement.

"Because," she said patiently, "you didn't shave for her, you did it for me. And I see you, Dane Garrett. I see you trying, and I love you even more for it."

"You ... you love me?"

The words clawed their way up my throat, excited and appalled.

"You shouldn't."

I sounded ungrateful, but that wasn't how I felt. Gratitude swelled inside me, blooming unashamedly, reaching toward her warmth.

"How are you so sure?" My voice cracked. "About me? About us?"

She smiled as if she'd unearthed the biggest secret in the world.

"Because the first time I read your words, I knew that you'd let me see behind the wall you'd built around your heart. And with each letter, each word that you wrote after that, I saw what a beautiful man you are ... in here."

And she laid her hand on my chest.

I didn't deserve her, I knew that, but if she'd let me, I'd spend my whole life proving the Becky's of the world wrong. Or rather, I'd earn Ella's love, drop by precious drop. And I hoped that would take me a lifetime.

She rested her head on my chest, and my arms wrapped around her, one hand tangled in the soft strands of her hair, the other protective on her back.

"Dane," she breathed, heating the bare skin at my neck. "Dane, take me home."

It was the first time we'd walked anywhere together, and it took a moment for our strides to match, Ella being so much shorter than me. But when we found our rhythm, I took a deep, quiet pleasure in her by my side, walking along the street, my arm around her shoulders.

I could have walked like that forever, the cold misting breaths, the warmth of her body against mine, the crunch of snow beneath our feet, everything completely ordinary and completely perfect.

I admit I was nervous as Ella let us into her building. I wanted her, God, I wanted her so badly. I was afraid it would be over too quickly, and of course thinking that made it almost certain to happen. When we'd fucked in the storage closet at Nottoway it had been fireworks, spontaneous combustion, and I hadn't had time to think about it, or even care about the consequences. But now ... yeah, whole different ballgame. It mattered so much that the tension felt like a concrete block had settled on my chest.

She smiled at me over her shoulder as she pushed the key into her front door.

"Go on in," she said.

Tense and uncomfortable, I walked down a narrow hallway. Everything smelled clean, and the biscuit-colored carpet hushed my footsteps.

I stopped in the living room, gazing at a space full of books, colorful with clutter. If a room can have feelings—and fuck knows they can, especially a cell—this room felt happy. It had a quiet joy that perfectly matched Ella.

A long, comfortable sofa faced a large, flat-screen TV, and three remote controls were lined up on a pine coffee table.

The kitchenette was small and tidy, with yellow painted cabinets, and an enormous white refrigerator.

I realized I was standing there like a bump on a log when Ella gave an embarrassed laugh.

"So, this is it!"

No, not embarrassed: she was nervous, too. And there was me acting like a fucking tool.

I pulled her into my arms, a reassuring word on my lips when she stared up at me.

That look, so full of hope and fear and expectation, it lit the blue touch paper, and I went from zero to sixty in the time it took my heart to pump hot blood around my body.

Need drove me, uncertainty reined me in, and my fingers trembled.

I closed my eyes, blindly groping towards her, and we met in a frenzy of lips and teeth and tongues and oh God, so good.

Hunger, intense hunger peeled away the fear, and I took my woman into her bedroom, crashing against unfamiliar furniture.

Laughing and gasping, she stripped me bare, pressing burning kisses to overheated skin. I didn't have the strength to fight my orgasm as it spewed against the soft skin of her belly. And when she dragged a finger through the dripping mess and sucked on it hard, my dick bucked against her hips, hardening again.

I'd never seen her breasts. They'd always been hidden by clothes and once by darkness. They filled my hands and I sucked on them thirstily, drinking down her moans and sighs, licking between the deep valley of her chest and biting the dusky nipples.

It was perfect and overwhelming and the scent of her skin made me want to howl at the moon. Smooth, satiny, scorching skin was mine for the taking, and I was a thief, stealing everything I could.

When my fingers explored the soft, wiry curls over her mound, my head exploded with pleasure. I licked and sucked, moonstruck crazy with the scent of her readiness. Her shuddering breaths, my name on her swollen lips was my victory and my reward.

And when I pushed her thighs apart and penetrated deeply, pressing my hand over her stomach to feel myself inside her, my thoughts flew away.

Her nails scored down my back, taking what was given freely, and we soared together in a heated, sweating, pool of pleasure.

I came inside her with a rush of heat and the most wonderful sensation that she'd broken me. I was hers.

We separated slowly, reveling in the fluids that glued us together, and I held her tightly because this was love and this was real, and my life would never be the same again. Ahead was sunlight and hope. So much hope.

Her breaths calmed to a slow and tender pace, complete and content.

"Let me count the ways I love thee."

I grinned at her, stretching out in her fucking amazing bed, soft sheets and softer pillows, soft skin resting on mine.

"Is that Shakespeare?"

"Close," she laughed. "It's from a poem by Elizabeth Barrett Browning, but she based it on Shakespeare's style."

"Teach me?"

Her eyes glowed with happiness.

"You really want to know?"

"You must love that poem to quote it, so yeah, I want to know." I looked at her seriously, cupping her sweet face in my rough hands. "I want to know everything that matters to you."

"*How do I love thee, Dane Garrett? Let me count the ways.*"

She ran her hands over my newly cut hair, then swept her fingers down my neck, chest, stomach and thighs.

"*I love thee to the depth and breadth and height my soul can reach,*" and she placed her cheek over my chest, listening to my thundering heart. "*When feeling out of sight for the ends of being and ideal grace.*"

She lifted her head and dusted soft fingerprints across my eyelids.

"*I love thee to the level of every day's most quiet need, by sun and candlelight.*" And she brushed my lips with the tips of her fingers. "*I love thee freely, as men strive for right.*"

My eyes opened as she ran her forefinger down my throat.

"*I love thee purely, as they turn from praise.*"

She kissed my temples, her lips pressing against my heated skin.

"*I love thee with the passion put to use in my old griefs, and with my childhood's faith.*"

She kissed my forehead, lingering lovingly.

"*I love thee with a love I seemed to lose with my lost saints.*"

And she lifted her head to seal a kiss against my lips.

"*I love thee with the breath, smiles, tears, of all my life; and, if God choose, I shall but love thee better after death.*" She smiled. "Which means forever, until death us do part."

And then she kissed away the tears that gathered in my eyes because I'd never known that the raging pain inside my heart was love tearing out all the bitterness, all the suffering, all the mistakes and bad choices. And I cried because this woman meant the world to me; she was my whole entire world, and always would be. And I cried because hope is belief, and she believed in me.

My God, she believed in me.

EPILOGUE

ELLA

It was a year before I saw Becky again. I think she'd been waiting to be proved right. But of course she wasn't.

For three months, Dane continued to live at Beacon House; that grim, gray building aptly named after all. He worked at the burger bar, serving cokes and fries and onion rings, smiling at customers, and learning how to be part of the world.

He earned his GED on the first attempt, and we celebrated by eating pizza in bed and drinking alcohol-free beer, loving freely and intensely.

He won over my parents, too. Not on the first visit, or the second, or even the third. In fact, I couldn't say when exactly it happened, but his quiet, determined love reassured them that he was a man of his word, and where he promised to love me forever, it was not a promise given lightly or easily, but a promise forged of tears and trial and facing all his fears.

And I took him to the ocean. He stood, staring, for the longest time, his eyes drifting shut as he felt the cool, salty spray on his cheeks. And then he kissed me, with the wide sky above us and sand between our toes. And the limitless horizon was our covenant to each other.

When three months was over and he was no longer a parolee, he moved into my apartment, filling the emptiness with his limitless love—and never once left wet towels on the floor. He needed very little to make him happy and measured each moment, reminding me that every small piece builds a larger picture. Snowflakes on my eyelashes, a patch of blue sky on a blustery day, he saw it all, and loved it all. And he loved me.

And there were bad days with rude customers and bills that were bigger than expected. There were difficult days when my job didn't go so well and I came home exhausted and in tears. And on those days I saw the rage in his eyes that made me tremble: not for me, but for him.

But with each day that tried us, the simple pleasure of holding each other's naked body at night, healed us, whether or not we made love.

And slowly we made friends, as a couple, meeting people who didn't care about the man Dane had been, only the magnificent person they saw before them. And he was magnificent. He stood taller and moved with pride and humility, and his endless kindness was matched only by his endless thirst for learning. Oh, the teacher in me rejoiced at that.

But he taught me so much, too. And I thank the Lord for the day that took me into Nottoway Correctional Facility, a bleak and sunless place. A hopeless, heartless place, where I found the love of my life.

We saw Becky in the street. We'd just come from visiting Hudson at Beacon House and had spent an afternoon making plans for his future.

Becky glanced, then glanced again, her eyes widening

with shock and surprise. Her gaze dropped to our linked hands, and I think I saw a small smile before she looked away. Although I may have imagined it.

Dane followed her with his eyes then turned to me, his fingers tightening on my hand, reassuring and certain.

And the warmth of his smile was worth every struggle we'd face, every setback, every sadness. Because we'd face them together. Student and teacher. Man and woman. Lover and loved.

Together.

THE END

REVIEWS

Reviews are love! Honestly, they are! But it also helps other people to make an informed decision before buying my book.

So I'd really appreciate if you took a few seconds to do just that :)

Thank you!

MORE ABOUT JHB

Jane Harvey-Berrick—that's me!—is the author of bestseller DANGEROUS TO KNOW & LOVE as well as stories of carnival life in THE TRAVELING SERIES, or if you like a bit more steam, you might want to try THE EDUCATION SERIES.

But if you enjoyed this story, and I hope you did, then you might like to look at LIFERS the story and suffering of Jordan Kane as he struggles with life on parole after release from prison.

I also writes about soldiers, surfers and ordinary people in smart, thoughtful, emotional contemporary romances.

My acclaimed novella PLAYING IN THE RAIN was featured in Huffington Post's list of Top Ugly Cry Reads! Click **here** to see the whole list.

And if you enjoy short stories, why not sign up to my newsletter? You'll receive a **free** short story each month.

You can sign up for my newsletter here.

MORE BOOKS BY JHB

Series Titles

*The Education Series

An epic love story spanning the years, through war zones and more...

*The Education of Sebastian (Education series #1)

*The Education of Caroline (Education series #2)

*The Education of Sebastian & Caroline (combined edition, books 1 & 2)

Semper Fi: The Education of Caroline (Education series #3)

*The Traveling Series

All the fun of the fair ... and two worlds collide

*The Traveling Man (Traveling series #1)

*The Traveling Woman (Traveling series #2)

*Roustabout (Traveling series #3)

*Carnival (Traveling series #4)

*Gypsy (Traveling series #5)

The Justin Trainer Series

The bodyguard and the billionaire

Guarding the Billionaire (Justin Trainer series #1)
Saving the Billionaire (Justin Trainer series #2)

* *The EOD Series*
Blood, bombs and heartbreak
*Tick Tock (EOD series #1)
* Bombshell (EOD series #2)

**The Rhythm Series*
Blood, sweat, tears and dance
*Slave to the Rhythm (Rhythm series #1)
*Luka (Rhythm series #2)

Standalone Titles
Contemporary Romance
The Lilac Cadillac
Battle Scars
One Careful Owner
*Lifers
At Your Beck & Call
The New Samurai
Exposure

New Adult
*Dangerous to Know & Love
Dazzled
Summer of Seventeen

Paranormal
*The Dark Detective: Venator (Book #1)
*The Dark Detective: Paukúnnum (Book #2)

Novellas
Playing in the Rain

*Behind the Walls

Anthologies of Short Stories
*The Year Book Volume 1
*The Year Book Volume 2
*The Year Book Volume 3

Audio Books
One Careful Owner
(*narrated by Seth Clayton*)

On the Stage
Later, After: Playscript
Trailer

With Alana Albertson
Father Figure

* These titles are published in languages other than English. Please check Jane's website for details—and receive **a free short story every month** when you sign up for her newsletter :)

QR code for Jane's website

ROMANCE WITH STUART REARDON

My love co-author with these titles

Two book series - contemporary romance

*Undefeated

*Model Boyfriend

Three book series - romcom

*Gym Or Chocolate?

*The World According to Vince

*The Baby Game

Standalone

Survivor Love Island *(romcom)*

*Touch My Soul *(novella)*

WRITING AS BERRICK FORD

Police Thrillers, UK

Dead Water
Dead Man's Dive
Dead Reckoning
Dead Shore

www.berrickford.com

www.ingramcontent.com/pod-product-compliance
Lightning Source LLC
Chambersburg PA
CBHW030640130626
46552CB00002B/947